AN URGENT MESSAGE OF WOWNESS

KAREN McCOMBIE

SCHOLASTIC

First published in the UK in 2007 by Scholastic Children's Books
An imprint of Scholastic Ltd
Euston House, 24 Eversholt Street
London, NW1 1DB, UK
Registered office: Westfield Road, Southam, Warwickshire, CV47 0RA

10 digit ISBN 0 439 95114 3
13 digit ISBN 978 0439 95114 2

British Library Cataloguing-in-Publication Data
A CIP catalogue record for this book is available from the British
Library

Typeset by M Rules
Printed and bound by GGP Media GmbH, Poessneck
Papers used by Scholastic Children's Books are made from wood
grown in sustainable forests.

1 3 5 7 9 10 8 6 4 2

www.scholastic.co.uk/zone

For my bunch of heathers . . .
Milly Heather (my sweetpea, my darling)
and Heather Doyle (my lovely mum-in-law)

A very big, huge, **MASSIVE** thanks to
Harriet Reed, who once sent me an email
with the heading "An Urgent Message of
Wowness" . . . where would I be without
her inspiration?

# Contents

# 20% random imperfectness

Let's skip way back. I mean *way* back.

Back to a school, ooh, about forever ago, where a beautiful sixteen-year-old girl meets a gorgeous seventeen-year-old boy. They're perfect together. After a few hard-studying, fun-travelling years, they get married and have two perfect children . . . and me.

OK, I've gone too far forward: let's rewind and stop at the point when my big brother joined the family.

Jo-Jo was born exactly one minute into the New Year. After a dramatic and exciting journey (he nearly made his first appearance in the back of a Ford Mondeo taxi), he finally burst into the world as fireworks spilled into the sky outside the labour ward. All the midwives and doctors and expectant mums and dads gave him and my proud parents three cheers and a round of applause.

Tallie's birth was wow in quite a different way: she was born at home, surrounded by candles, soft music and minimal yelling (Mum says). Me and Jo-Jo were conveniently asleep, dreaming of skateboards (Jo-Jo) and lost toys (me), unaware that our kid sister was slipping into the world via the spare room, to the scent of vanilla and rose and the sound of Dido's "No Angel".

In between Jo-Jo and Tallie there was me (I was saving the worst for last). Dad was in bed with a basin by his side and a bad case of gastric flu when Mum announced that her contractions had started. He thought she was just joking – it *was* 1st April after all. I think even as an unborn baby, I realized that having April Fool's Day as a birthday was going to be less than fun. In an effort to avoid a lifetime's worth of teasing, I dug my tiny heels in and tried hard to hang on till the 2nd, but the midwife was having none of it. I was dragged out by ventouse (a fancy name for the suction cup attached to my head) at 11.45 p.m.

Dad arrived, grey-faced, from his twentieth visit to the hospital bathroom to find an exhausted wife and a pointy-headed alien instead of the rosy-cheeked daughter he was expecting.

I'm Heather, by the way. Heather P. Smith. I like people to guess what the "P" stands for, then infuriate them by not telling. Adding a little mystery is the only way to make my dull name interesting.

I'm the middle child of the perfect Smith family. Well, statistically speaking, the eighty per cent perfect Smith family, with me mucking things up with my twenty per cent random imperfectness. It's not that I look like an alien any more (the pointy-headed swelling went down a week or two after my parents brought me home), but compared to Mum and Dad and Jo-Jo and Tallie, I'm a bit un-wow. Imagine a drift of elegant swans gliding along a river, with a yellow plastic duck in their midst; or a pride of majestic, athletic lions prowling the African plains, with a wombat waddling along behind them. I *am* that rubber duck; I *am* that wombat.

Wombat's my email name, by the way. Well, calling myself heathersmith@hotmail.co.uk would be pretty dull, plus there're probably a zillion Heather Smiths out there. (Thanks, Mum and Dad, for giving me a name that can't be shortened to anything funky.)

Wombat's a lousy nickname, I know. I thought it could be a cool email name, in a quirky kind of way, but I'm just really bad at getting excited about stuff and then realizing down the line that I had less of a moment of genius and more of a judder of dumbness.

I nearly went with "Scooter" for my email address, the nickname that Jo-Jo gave me when I was born. Mum and Dad had bought my four-year-old brother a shiny silver scooter as a consolation prize, to make up for ruining his childhood by bringing a squalling baby into his life. He couldn't pronounce "Heather", so he stuck to calling me after his much-preferred present.

Jo-Jo. . . Luckily, he liked me a lot more once I grew up and out of the random crying and pooey nappies stage. He never seems to mind that I walk a wobbly line between cool and nerdy.

Tallie loves me too, even though I regularly ruin her "let's pretend!!" games by being a useless shopkeeper/ ballet teacher/fairy princess/pet puppy or whatever. It's not that I'm not imaginative – Mum once said that if imagination worked on a scale of one-to-ten, I'd be forty-two – it's just that my mind goes blank when I'm faced with a basket of plastic fruit/an overload of pink frills/fairy wands/I'm being ordered to bark. My cluttered brain isn't wired for all that stuff.

Speaking of Mum – and Dad, of course – I know they both love me, even if I confuse them. I mean, they're pretty straightforward: Dad is a dentist who likes golfing, reading current affairs magazines and buying box sets of DVDs off the internet. Mum helps out in her friend's posh clothes shop, and spends most of what she earns buying posh clothes from the shop. They know where they are with Jo-Jo: he does karate, plays squash for the school team and listens to indie music, when he isn't busy being hyper-intelligent and handsome and lusted over by every girl in the known universe (especially my pretty perfect best friend, Becca).

And Tallie. . . She's just the whole ultra-cute package: sweet, polite, with a bedroom packed full of fairy bits, fluffy bobs and bunting, and with a tendency to hold dolls' tea parties at every opportunity.

"Stop making yourself sound like a freak!" Becca would say, if she saw this stuff. And no, I guess I'm not a freak. I guess it's just the fact that my whole family – and Becca, for that matter – seems to know exactly *who* they are, and exactly *what* they like.

But not me.

I've always had interests and hobbies as often as colds (and I get colds a *lot*). And then I'll get over them, and haven't a clue why I felt so completely passionate about them at the time. I mean, *why* was I so obsessed with always spotting yellow cars when I was two? (OK, it was something to do with a rhyme with a fish in a Dr Seuss book that I loved.)

Still, that was only the *start* of it.

I got into collecting keyrings (a small collection: I stopped at three), collecting lost soft toys left on pavements (got fifty-one, and still collecting), wearing only boys' shoes (between the ages of six and eight), cutting out Gary Larson *Far Side* cartoons from newspapers (drove my dad mad if he was still physically reading the paper at the time), star-gazing (the telescope I got for my eleventh birthday is good for hanging jewellery off now), turning vegan (I missed smoky bacon crisps too much), spending two years begging my mum for an auricle* piercing (when she finally stopped saying no and told me I could when I was fourteen, I realized I'd already lost interest), taking books and stuff to school in carrier bags from hip shops (i.e. record shops and clothes shops, not Tesco's), becoming besotted with the idea of travelling round South America (lasted till I read that quite a few South American countries have a problem with gangs kidnapping foreigners for ransom money).

And it didn't just start with spotting yellow cars and end with me wanting to back-pack round countries I might get abducted in. My stupid habit of collecting hobbies and interests (and often dumping them again) goes on and endlessly on. My latest is scouring *The British Book of Hit Singles and Albums*. Or more precisely, scouring *The British Book of Hit Singles and Albums* for songs with really bizarre titles. (Get this: under "A" alone there are three excellently weird-sounding songs: "And A Bang On The Ear"; "Ain't Gonna Bump No More (With No Big Fat Woman)"; and "All Around My Hat". I'm going to download them later and see what on earth they sound like.)

* Look it up on the internet. Warning: it might make you go "bleurghhh".

Ah, now . . . d'you see what I mean about me having a cluttered brain? Can you imagine how often my patient, perfect family smile and nod, listening to me happily rant on about things they know I'll be bored of by a week on Tuesday?

Ah . . . my patient, perfect family.

Let's get back to them.

'Cause lots of what I've just told you about my family isn't exactly true. I mean, it *was* true, in the past (i.e., rewind to a few months ago), but it's definitely not so true now. That's because the general perfectness of my branch of the Smiths came to an end on Monday 26 March.

It ended with a bombshell.

When I say bombshell, I mean the "NOOOOO – IT CAN'T BE TRUE!!" type, not the ka-***boom*** type.

But it was still big enough to make my whole family implode, explode, go right round the bend and back again.

And by the time I got my cluttered brain around it all, I realized that being twenty per cent imperfect was perfectly fine – compared to the rest of the screwballs I was related to. . .

| From: | **wombat** |
| Subject: | **Tracklisting** |
| Date: | **Tuesday 27 March** |
| To: | **rsmith@smiledentalgroup** |

Dad –

Can you print this out? It goes with the CD I stuck in your bag when you weren't looking. I did the same CD for everyone; I spent ages sussing out the tracks and downloading them off i-Tunes. I thought it would be a nice surprise, but I guess YOUR surprise sort of blew mine out of the water. By about a zillion miles. . .
   Hope you like it.
   Love,
   Heather x


**Number Ones From The British Charts On The Days We Were All Born!**
Compiled by Heather P. Smith

- "Something In The Air" Thunderclap Newman (Rory Smith, born 14 July 1969)
- "Woodstock" Matthew's Southern Comfort (Joanna May Smith, born 12 November 1970)
- "Do They Know It's Christmas?" Band Aid II (Jonathan Joseph Smith, born 1 January 1990)
- "Doop Doop" (Heather P. Smith, born 1 April 1994)

- "Evergreen" Will Young
  (Tallulah Belle Smith, born 9 March 2002)
- "Things Can Only Get Better" D:Ream
  (Rebecca Clare Fitzgerald, born 7 February
  1994)

# The missing exclamation mark

OK, it's rewind time again.

Not *too* far back.

Just a short swirl back. The time is now exactly ten minutes to The Bombshell.

Of course, none of us knew it was ten minutes to The Bombshell, or we wouldn't have been doing all the dumb, ordinary stuff we were doing. Probably.

"Doop-doop-de-doop!"

I think Becca hoped she looked cute and perky, doing the Charleston over by the CD player.

(*Charleston*: a dance from the 1920s, involving lots of foot-flicking and knee-knocking. Did you know there was also a dance in the 1960s called the Frug? And another one called the Mashed Potato? And one in the 1990s called Big Fish, Little Fish, Cardboard Box? Seriously?! Dancing is obviously for crazy people. Which is why I do it all the time – in the privacy of my bedroom, where big brothers can't walk in on you.)

"God, what *is* this rubbish?" moaned Jo-Jo, suddenly slouching into the living room. As he walked, he was doing this stretch he always does, holding an elbow up to one ear, reaching across with his other hand and pulling his arm tight, so the lean muscles strained above his T-shirt sleeve.

It was a sight that made Becca go weak at the knees

and most other places. Mind you, if he *burped*, it would have the same effect on her, she was so crazy about him.

She never told me that stuff for sure, but when you've been best friends with someone for four years, you can read their minds at certain moments. And I was able to read all that longing for Jo-Jo due to the fact that Becca always forgot to breathe for a few seconds, the minute Jo-Jo walked in the room. It was the way her eyes fixed on him like magnets, same as three-year-old kids in the park get transfixed over other little kids holding ice cream. The yearning just radiates out of them.

Maybe one of these days, Becca would want to admit to all the yearning to me. But for that moment, she just held her breath, locked her eyes on my brother, and stopped mid-Charleston, pink-cheeked.

"It's not *rubbish!*" I said, looking up from the tracklisting I was carefully writing out in gold pen. "It's a present for *you*! For everyone!"

I picked up a plastic CD case and tossed it at him. I'd burned a CD for me, one for Becca, one for Jo-Jo, one for Mum (to play in the house), one for Dad (to play in the car or his surgery), one for Tallie (who was using hers as a makeshift picnic table that all her smallest dolls were huddled round just now, having tea).

"'Number Ones From The British Chart On The Days We Were All Born!'" Jo-Jo read out. "S'not a bad idea."

Yay! Jo-Jo thought I'd had a not bad idea! I claim a miracle. . .

"Just a pity all the tracks are so lousy," he added, flicking his eyes down the gold lettering inside the plastic casing.

He was grinning, not growling, so I didn't take offence.

Anyway, I knew the tracks weren't so much lousy, as pretty odd together. The first two (for Dad and Mum's birthdays) sounded sort of hippy-ish. Jo-Jo's was one of the most famous charity records ever (though it was a bit unseasonal – a Christmas record in March, I mean). Tallie's was soppy but nice, and Becca's was a dancey, singalong, sort of thing.

"And this – *this* one is *deeply* lousy!"

The track for *my* birthday: a band called Doop doing a song called "Doop", which was just an updated version of some old music people did the Charleston too. According to the *British Book of Hit Singles and Albums*, they were Dutch. Maybe they had lots more records out in Holland but I think they only put out this one, kind of fluffy, silly novelty single in Britain.

A fluffy, silly novelty single: that's exactly right for an April Fool's Day Number One. I couldn't have had anything classy or brilliant for my birthday, could I?

"I like it," said Tallie, not looking up from the intricate game she was playing. Tallie always played intricate, dainty games. Pretty quiet ones too. Mum hugged her a lot – probably 'cause she was thrilled to have the sort of small daughter who enjoyed wearing hair clips and staying clean, after one that thought muddy puddles were the best invention ever and tore holes in the knees of every pair of stripy tights whenever she went out to play (sorry, Mum).

"Yeah, *'course* you like it – you're five, you've got no taste yet!" said Jo-Jo, tapping Tallie affectionately on the head with his CD.

"Hey!" Tallie growled like a slightly irked kitten. "Anyway, Krystyna likes it too."

Me and Jo-Jo glanced through to the conservatory off the living room, and saw Krystyna shaking her bum in time to the music as she dusted.

Krystyna is our cleaner. She's been our cleaner for about a year, since Mum said she was too busy working to faff around with hoovering and whatever. Yeah, three afternoons a week wafting around an expensive clothes shop sounds exhausting, I know. My mum is lovely and everything, but at the time I wished she would just be honest and say she *hated* hoovering and all that housework stuff.

And if *I* was being honest, Krystyna made me kind of edgy. She was usually done and dusted and gone by the time we got home from school on a Monday afternoon. But sometimes – like today – she was running late, or being extra, especially clean or something, and she'd be here, in a spookily silent, non-smiling way. I mean, we got a polite "hello" for sure, but no more than that. Fair enough, I knew she was Polish – or maybe it was Estonian – and perhaps didn't speak much English. But she didn't even go smiley and gushy over Tallie, and *everyone* went smiley and gushy over Tallie, 'cause of her exceptional levels of cuteness. Or maybe it was my fault; maybe her silence was brooding resentment over having to clean my room. What with all my piles of books and mags and collections of stuff lurking around, it wasn't like it was exactly a breeze to clean.

"Where's Mum?" asked Jo-Jo suddenly. "Isn't it tea time yet?"

Jo-Jo eats like a horse. A sleek, prize-winning racehorse, of course.

"She's upstairs, having a shower," I reminded him. Mum *always* had a shower when she came home from work, like she was a miner washing off a day's coal-dust or something (more like a half-day's worth of heady perfumes off posh customers). "Anyway, it's ages till tea time. It's only quarter to five."

"Should-I-make-some-toast?" Becca said in a garbled rush.

I think she'd just remembered to start breathing again. The helium-squeak voice always happened whenever she was suffering from Jo-Jo-induced oxygen deprivation.

"Mmm, please! Peanut butter and blackcurrant jam on mine!" I said, glancing up from my gold scribbling.

"You weirdo!" Jo-Jo laughed at me. "Just butter on mine, Becca."

"'Just butter on mine, *thanks*, Becca'," I prompted him, kind of enjoying getting something over on my brother, even if it was just a little light teasing over a lost thank you.

"*Thanks*, Becca!" Jo-Jo repeated, smiling her way.

Becca tucked her shiny, brown hair self-consciously behind her ears and blushed prettily.

"Sure . . . um, Tallie? You want some?"

In the full beam of Jo-Jo's gaze, Becca temporarily forgot that Tallie didn't eat anything that involved random crumbs.

"No, thank you," Tallie answered, leaning over and placing tiny china plates of painted china cake in front of her matching Polly Pocket dolls.

As Becca wafted out of the room on a high, Jo-Jo pulled a rolled-up music magazine out of his back pocket and flopped down on one of our two huge squashy sofas.

Jo-Jo reading, me scribbling, Tallie doing her doll-thing, with a bit of dumb *Doop*-ing going on in the background. It was all kind of normal. It was all just as it should be.

Till we heard the front door open, an hour and a quarter earlier than it *usually* opened.

*(Countdown: five minutes to The Bombshell.)*

"Daddy!" yelped Tallie, jumping up and skipping through to the hall.

Dad? Already? He always drilled, filled and polished till five-ish, then methodically tidied up at the dental surgery before he headed home for six o'clock and tea time. I looked at my watch. The kitsch kitten on the face looked back at me, as if it was about to miaow, "Yep, I *am* telling the right time, before you ask!".

I glanced over at Jo-Jo, but he was engrossed in his magazine.

"Hi, guys. . ." said Dad, appearing in the living-room doorway with Tallie limpeted to his chest.

All of a sudden, the universe seemed just one fraction of a centimetre off-kilter. Everything looked, sounded and seemed the same, but somehow . . . *wasn't*.

Yeah, it was to do with the hour-and-quarter early thing, definitely. But it was also 'cause of the way Dad had just said his usual "Hi, guys!" hello. The telltale *wrongness* was the lack of exclamation mark: it was missing from his voice. (Trust me, there's a pretty noticeable difference between a "Hi, guys!" and a "Hi, guys. . .".)

Add the time and the exclamation mark wrongnesses to the fact that Dad's face was contradicting itself – his hundred-watt smile was glinting our way, but his eyes looked like they'd just seen a mouthful of teeth that hadn't been near a toothbrush in several years – and it meant Something Was Up, I was sure.

"Mum around?" Dad asked, smile wide, eyes glazed.

Was his grey-flecked brown hair slightly tousled, like he'd been running his hand through it? Dad *never* did tousled. *No one* in my family did tousled hair, except me. It was like they all had in-built wind, weather and tousling immunity. I was a wind, weather and tousling *magnet*. I could get a tangle in newly washed and brushed hair just by turning my head slightly to the left.

"Mum's in the shower," Tallie told him. "Let's go up and surprise her!"

"You stay here, honey," said Dad, easing Tallie down to the creamy beige carpet. "I've just got to pop upstairs and have a word with her."

Tallie didn't moan, like most little kids would've. She just gazed up at Dad and then went quietly back to her mini tea party.

As he headed up the stairs, I glanced down at the gold lettering in front of me and tried to get my brain to stop jangling and focus. It wouldn't.

"Dad doesn't usually finish work till later," I said out loud, testing to see if Jo-Jo would come up with a confident, logical answer to my statement.

"Maybe everyone had perfect teeth today," he muttered, not looking up from his magazine.

"Perfect teeth!" trilled Tallie, turning and baring hers, so I got a ravishing glimpse of two rows of baby pearly whites.

"Hmm. . ." I mumbled, scratching my nose.

I don't usually have nervous tics or anything, but when something's making my head jangle, I tend to rub and scratch my nose about a hundred zillion times, even though it's not in the least bit itchy.

And *boy*, was I suddenly rubbing and scratching it now.

Jo-Jo was still reading; Tallie was still doing her doll thing. Maybe my head was jangling over nothing. Except Krystyna. . . I spotted Krystyna through the open French doors, pausing, stone-still, Mr Sheen in hand. She was gazing up at the ceiling, listening.

Mum and Dad's bedroom window was just above there.

"D'you still need a hand with that maths homework you were talking about, Heather?" Jo-Jo suddenly asked, as he flicked through pages of posturing and posing bands.

"Yeah, please. Um, later, though. . ." I mumbled gloomily.

I wasn't gloomy 'cause he'd offered to help – it's, like, *amazing* to have a brainbox big brother who offers to help you with your homework and everything – it was just the thought of sitting down and staring at stuff that made as much sense as ancient Babylonian, even *with* a brainbox brother trying to help you decode it.

"You've said 'later' for the last three days," said Jo-Jo, grinning at me.

"Yeah, well."

Yeah, well, I was a genius at putting things off (and getting an ulcer over it), same as Jo-Jo was a genius at breezing through homework and exams like they were a complete doddle.

"Maybe *I* can help you too, Heather," said Tallie. "My teacher said today I have *excellent* handwriting."

I think my little sister was single-handedly bankrupting her school, her teacher had to order in so many extra sheets of gold stars, just for her. *My* best subject aged five was eating school dinners.

"That's OK, thanks, Tal—"

I stopped, mid-name. Tallie didn't seem to notice me stopping – she was too busy repositioning a Polly Pocket that had toppled headfirst into her china pudding – or notice the noise that had made me stop in the first place.

The clomping of heavy footsteps, up above.

Jo-Jo hadn't noticed either, his eyes glued to some album review or whatever.

But Krystyna had. Like me, her eyes were following the footsteps, from the bedroom over our heads to the hall landing, over to the left.

*Blam, blam, blam, blam!* mirrored by a *stomp, stomp, stomp, stomp!* as two sets of feet thundered down the stairs.

*Everyone* looked up, as the door burst open.

For a millisecond, Mum stood alone in the doorway. At least I *thought* it was Mum, but I'd never seen her look so . . . kerfuffled. It was as if she'd been splurged out of a tumble dryer halfway through a spin cycle.

"It's fine. It's all right," Dad said quickly, appearing behind Mum. He wasn't talking to her, but to us. He must've slotted into protective, reassuring Dad mode, seeing our stunned faces.

"Excuse *me*, Rory!" Mum yelped, turning to stare at him sharply. "In what way is it 'fine'?! How is it 'all right'?"

Bundled in a big, fluffy bath towel, she was damp, white-faced, with a second, teetering towel piled and twisted around her head. Wisps of wet blonde hair were plastered to her neck. It's funny how you notice stupid details at weird times, but I suddenly spotted that two of her neat, tasteful fake nails had pinged off. *Where were they?* my idiot brain fretted, as if it was in the least bit important.

"Joanna, let's go upstairs and talk about this some more," my dad implored.

"And say what? Do you want to drop your bombshell again? Just in case I didn't get it the first time?"

"Bombshell?" said Jo-Jo. "What 'bombshell'?"

(*Here it comes, very nearly.*)

"Better tell them, don't you think?" Mum fumed, on the edge of tears.

I'd never seen her like this. OK, so I saw her dab her eyes at the end of sad films, or cry softly at charity ads on TV, sniffing as she copied down the donations numbers flashing up on the screen.

But I'd never seen her this bizarre: trembling and

shaking and looking like she might crumple or punch someone – one or the other.

Dad looked at her pleadingly, opened his mouth to speak, and then closed it again. He dropped his head down for a second – a second that felt like a year – and when he lifted it back up, he was looking at me, Jo-Jo and Tallie.

"Well, I—"

(*Get ready. . .*)

"Your dad's leaving us!" Mum burst in before he could speak.

Crying. Shouting. Pleading. Questioning. Even lashing out. Me and my brother and sister could've done any of those, in the circumstances.

Instead, Jo-Jo and Tallie turned into silent, staring statues.

Me? I did exactly the wrong thing, naturally.

It was the towel sliding sideways on Mum's head, like a melting whirly ice-cream cone.

It was Becca standing frozen in embarrassment behind my parents in the hallway, with a plate in one hand, and a bite of toast bulging, hamster-style, in her cheek.

It was a sideways glance towards the conservatory, where Krystyna was covering her mouth with a duster, as if she was trying to hide herself in the most useless way possible.

It was the fact that I caught sight of my reflection in a pane of glass in the French window and saw that after rubbing my nose five zillion times in the last few minutes, I now had gold ink smeared all over it.

It was Dad stutteringly apologizing to me in particular, saying he was sorry this had happened right before my birthday, as if stupid birthdays on stupid April Fool's Day mattered at a time like this.

It was all of those things – plus sheer shock – that made me burst out laughing. . .

**From:** wombat

**Subject:** Um . . . sorry

**Date:** Wednesday 28 March

**To:** rsmith@smiledentalgroup

Hi Dad –

Just wanted to say sorry for laughing the other day. When you were leaving, I mean. I think it was just nerves . . . like that time you took us to the theatre to see *The Lion King* and I got the giggles when I knew Simba's dad was about to get killed. Do you remember? I wish I didn't. That woman sitting behind us didn't stop tutting for ages, did she?

Anyway, have you listened to your CD yet? Maybe you don't have a CD player where you are. But you could still play it in the car, I guess, or in your CD player in the surgery, when you're back at work. (Mum said she spoke to your receptionist, who said you were taking some time off. But you *are* picking up your emails, somehow, somewhere, right?)

By the way, I think I might sound quite normal in this email, but I don't feel very normal.

Do you?

Where are you, Dad?

Love

Heather x

# The elephant in the corner

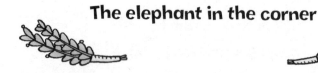

Fast forward to a week later.

"Tallie, you've hardly eaten your breakfast!" I said with a frown, staring at the bowl full of soggy flakes on the round, pine table.

"It tastes yeuccchhh," growled Tallie, padding out of the kitchen in her bunny-patterned pyjamas, dragging Mr Boo – her favourite teddy – along the ground behind her.

I'd been sort of banking on the fact that Tallie's five-year-old tastebuds wouldn't be sophisticated enough to figure out that I'd watered down the milk. Ha. Well, *I* didn't know we'd run out so soon – I bought a whole carton yesterday.

Speaking of yesterday . . . it was a very special day in the life of *me*. A day that I'm usually never allowed to forget. But every cloud has a silver lining, and in our house, that meant Dad's Bombshell had at least made everyone (except Becca) conveniently forget that yesterday was my birthday. Hurray! No April Fool's jokes on me for one, blissful year.

I celebrated – alone – by eating half the giant Toblerone that Becca gave me, and dancing round my room to the Top 40 Countdown on Radio One.

"Tallie," I called after my little sister, "we've got to leave for school in about ten minutes. Can you put some clothes on and brush your hair?"

"Where's my hairbrush?" she called back.

"Um, I'll have a look for it," I shouted, quickly opening the fridge, since that's where I'd found it yesterday, for no particular reason.

Nope, not there.

Urgh, everything felt so rushed and chaotic this morning. And the reason it all felt so rushed and chaotic was that Mum was a bit late getting out of bed – about seven days late, in fact.

She'd gone to bed about two hours after The Bombshell (i.e. about an hour and a half after Dad left with his suitcase haphazardly crammed) and hadn't got up since. Well, I guess that wasn't entirely true; we knew she got up to use the loo, since occasionally we'd hear a distant flushing. But apart from that, nada.

Nada is Spanish for nothing, in case you didn't know. And it felt like we'd been living in a great big bubble of nada for the last week. We'd heard precisely nothing from Dad. And Mum was saying precisely nothing except, "Thanks, but I'm not hungry" and "I promise I'll be OK soon, just give me a little bit of time".

As for me, Jo-Jo and Tallie, we were saying pretty much nothing too, except for "Can you get some milk on the way home?", "Anyone know how this defrost button works on the microwave?" and "Got your school lunch money?". (I was daily giving thanks to the god of school lunches – at least we would all get a smattering of vitamins that way.)

Honestly, it was like we were living with an elephant in the corner.

I guess I'd heard that saying before, but never got it

till now. It was all about a big, unspoken something between people, a big, unspoken something that's just like having an elephant hunched in the corner of your room, only everyone pretends it's not there.

And here we were – me and my brother and sister – ridiculously not mentioning the fact that Dad had left home and Mum had gone into hibernation in a *big* way.

In fact, I'd had enough of it.

"Hi," said Jo-Jo, slouching his way downstairs and into the kitchen, and dumping his canvas school bag on the worktop.

Time to talk elephants. Kind of.

"Jo-Jo. . .?"

"Uh-huh?"

"I just need. . ."

Urgh. This was harder than I thought. Where do you start with something so humungous? (I'm talking about my dad leaving here, not elephants.)

Should I start with The Bombshell night, when he blurted out all that stuff to Mum in front of us; all that "It's-not-you-it's-me" stuff and "There's-no-one-else-I-just-need-to-do-this-for-myself" waffle that didn't make much sense to any of us then, and still didn't make much sense a week later?

(I suddenly had a vision of Becca scrabbling around at the coat rack in the hall. I'd thought at first she'd been attempting to hide behind Mum's raincoat and Tallie's spotty duffle, then I realized she was just trying to leave as subtly as she could. Hard, when she put her arm through her jacket sleeve, while still clutching toast. . .)

Or maybe I should begin with Mum. Mum, who'd spent her last hour and a half prior to hibernation being comforted in the conservatory by Krystyna, who – it turned out – knew *lots* of English words. In fact, her so-far-hidden knowledge of the English language was pretty extensive. As she hugged Mum, she used an impressively wide selection of colourful phrases that she hurled after my dear, departing dad. (I got the distinct feeling that some "twisted, coward of a dog of a man!" might have done something similar to Krystyna down the line. . .)

Or maybe I should just come out and say I was feeling terrible, like I'd been picked up by a twister, same as Dorothy in *The Wizard of Oz*, and been splatted down in a world that I didn't quite recognize. Only this one wasn't *nearly* as attractive as Dorothy's. Instead of Technicolor, there was just our bland beige walls, and in place of a Yellow Brick Road there was a trail of rubbish that hadn't quite made it into the silver, flip-top bin.

"What do you need?" asked Jo-Jo, reaching into a kitchen drawer and pulling out a stash of money he'd put himself in charge of. "Bin-bags, right? And beans – we should get more beans and I'll do tea again tonight."

"I'm not talking about beans," I sighed. "I just need to talk to you about . . . y'know."

Y'know.

How lame was I? How much of a coward was I that I couldn't even say, y'know, *stuff* out loud to my own brother?

But Jo-Jo got it. He stopped counting the notes in his hand and looked up at me.

"I don't want to talk about him. I don't want to *think* about him. I just want to blank him out. OK, Heather?"

It didn't seem like Jo-Jo even wanted to call "him" Dad.

"But. . ."

I wasn't sure what I planned to say after "but" . . . I just knew I didn't want to stay saying nothing about the situation for *another* week.

"Look – he's made it pretty clear he doesn't care about us. So if he wants to take off with *whoever*, then that's fine. We've just got to forget about him like he's already forgotten about us."

"Huh?" I squeaked, thinking that I seemed to have missed a very important part of a conversation somewhere along the line. "But Dad didn't take off with someone! He said—"

"—there was no one else. Yeah, *yeah*," Jo-Jo snarled. "Well, if I had a thousand pounds, I'd bet on that being a big, fat *lie*."

Oh, so Jo-Jo was just *guessing*.

"Why d'you think that?" I asked him in surprise (after all, *I* was meant to be the one with the over-active imagination).

"'Cause him and Mum haven't been rowing, have they? And maybe if they'd been rowing all the time, then yeah, one of them might decide before the other one that it wasn't working out. One of them might come up with all that 'there's no-one-else-I-just-need-to-do-this' stuff."

He had a point. Mum and Dad *never* rowed. They went out for dinner. Dad always said Mum looked great when she swirled around in another expensive dress she didn't need. They'd just been talking about booking a gîte in France for our summer holidays.

"And why hasn't he called any of us?!" Jo-Jo added, on a roll now.

"I . . . I . . . don't know."

Something was suddenly nudging into my head, making it hard to think straight. I mean, would Mum and Dad end up getting divorced, like Kelise from my class's parents had? It happened last year, and she was so miserable she ended up going to a counsellor. Was that what was going to happen to me and Jo-Jo and Tallie? (*Calm down*, I told my over-active imagination. *He's only been gone a few days. They might get back together – people do.*)

"Well, *I* know!" Jo-Jo burst into my thoughts. "He's so loved up with someone else, and obviously feeling so tangled up in guilt 'cause he lied to us, that he hasn't had the bottle to phone. See?"

OK, I kind of did see. I didn't want to, 'cause it didn't fit in with the version of Dad in my head (kind, straightforward, easy-going), but I couldn't figure out any other excuse for the lack of phone calls or the fact that he hadn't got back to either of my emails. In fact, for a millionth of a microsecond, I kind of . . . well, I kind of *wished he was dead*.

Mad, huh?

But I didn't mean it in an I-really-hate-him way; it's just for that millionth of a microsecond it felt like it might not have *hurt* so much.

Dad being tragically killed by some freak lightning bolt

five minutes after leaving us seemed less heart-twistingly harsh than the idea of him swanning off with some gorgeous girly and instantly wiping his perfect family (plus me) from his mind.

But yeah, Jo-Jo's slant on The Bombshell was probably more accurate and a lot less grim than mine. And with logic like that, you can see why Jo-Jo was the boy genius of our family and I was the cluttered-brained ditz. . .

*Bleep-bleep, bleep-bleep. . .*

"I'll get it," said Jo-Jo, stretching across and grabbing the phone off the kitchen wall.

No sooner had he picked it up than he slammed it down again.

"Who was it?" I asked.

"Wrong number," he shrugged, striding to the other side of the kitchen, pulling open the fridge door and grabbing a carton of orange juice.

He shook it, felt it was empty, and threw it forcefully at the closed bin. It pinged off and landed with a soft thud next to the rest of the litter on the floor.

I would definitely need to buy bin-bags today.

"What are you two talking about?" a small voice suddenly asked from the doorway.

"Never mind that – what are you *wearing*?" I asked in return (and in a certain amount of shock), as I stared at Tallie.

Shiny shoes, flowery tights, flared denim skirt, pink long-sleeved T-shirt. It was business as usual – if you didn't count the scribbled black splodge covering the front of her top.

"It was boring and plain," said Tallie, dropping her chin to look at her artwork. "And I like hedgehogs."

The phone blasted into life again, so I didn't have time to ask where Tallie had got the black marker pen that she was still clutching in her hand.

"Do something with your hair!" I ordered her quickly, spotting the time on the kitchen wall clock as I snatched up the receiver.

"Hello?"

(*Please take that pen off her before she draws any hedgehog mates on her sleeves*, I silently willed Jo-Jo.)

"Heather?"

Ker-chunk – the sound of my heart stalling.

"Dad?" I said, in the teeny-tiniest of voices.

"Your brother just put the phone down on me. Can I speak to him?"

Fat chance. All I could see of Jo-Jo this second was his back, and a hand held up in the air in the international sign for "No way".

"Um . . . he just left for school," I lied.

"Oh. Right. Well, how are you all?"

Beyond awful.

"OK," I lied some more.

Why was I lying? I didn't know. It was just some stupid, unaccountable knee-jerk reaction, same as when I burst out laughing, right after Dad dropped The Bombshell.

("It's Dad!" I mouthed at Tallie. Tallie stuck her tongue out at the phone and scuttled off.)

"How's your mum?"

Part of me wanted to tell him that she was trapped

under her duvet by a hundredweight of gloom, in the hope that he'd swoop back and sort out this whole mess, like it had never happened. But something made me want to protect my mum. I didn't want her to sound all pathetic, even though she was definitely pathetic with a capital "P" right now.

"OK."

"Can I talk to her?"

"I don't think so."

(Mum wasn't capable of holding a bowl of watery soup at the moment, never mind a conversation with the husband that had just left her.)

"I see," said Dad stoically, though he didn't have a clue, really.

Hmm, maybe it was time I got brave and talked elephants with my dad.

"Did you get my emails?" I asked, in an annoyingly timid squeak.

"Yes. Yes, I did, Heather. Thanks. Just not had time to answer them."

Hmm . . . that was a bit vague.

"Dad, where are you staying?"

"Oh, that's not important right now," he said, even more vaguely.

His maddening vagueness made me imagine him lying on a sofa, being hand-fed hot buttered croissant by some woman we didn't even *know*. (And thanks, Jo-Jo, for helping make that image pop into my head.)

"Dad, why did you leave?

"Listen, I've got to go. . ."

But I was suddenly only half-listening; I'd just caught a sideways glimpse of Tallie posing in front of the hall mirror, with a tub of Jo-Jo's hair gel in her hand. Her fringe was currently standing straight up in a fin.

"I've got to go too, Dad," I said in a fluster, wondering how to solve Tallie's hair trauma in the three seconds we had before we had to zoom off to school.

"I'm . . . I'm so sorry, Heather."

"Huh?" The phone was temporarily held away from my ear, as I frantically tried waving my arm at Tallie to get her attention.

"I'll be in touch soon, I promise," I heard Dad saying, distant already, as if he was already in the process of putting the phone down. "By the way, happy birthday for yesterday. I promise I'll make it up to you when I get a chance. Bye, honey. . ."

As the phone went dead, my heart went *twinge*, which by some amazing biological chain reaction immediately sent tears of self-pity zooming in the direction of my eyeballs.

But they immediately retreated in shock when I saw Tallie spin her head round to stare at me.

"I like ladybirds too," she said simply, of the black-dotted, red-lipsticked blob on her left cheek.

Help.

What excuse could I give my form teacher for being late for school today?

"I'm sorry, Miss Hardy, but gremlins abducted my nice, cute, well-behaved sister and swapped her for one of their own. . ."

Nah, she'd never believe that. Maybe I should say

something more direct, like, "Sorry, but my family has unexpectedly unravelled".

The unravelling Smith family. How was it ever going to get fixed?

Anyone know where I could get a giant, family-sized plaster. . .?

**From:** wombat

**Subject:** Funny (but not ha-ha)

**Date:** Monday 2 April

**To:** rsmith@smiledentalgroup


Hi Dad

It was really nice to hear your voice this morning. Sorry if I sounded kind of funny (not ha-ha), but everything is sort of normal but a bit funny (not ha-ha) at home right now.

An example of seriously funny (not ha-ha): Tallie is now eating beans on toast. Yes – I know! "Toast is too crumb-y and beans are too orangey and messy!" Well, she's not saying that any more, specially not as she's stuffing it in her mouth.

By the way, I haven't told Mum you called. Don't think she's, um, up for talking at the moment.

And I don't think Jo-Jo's exactly ready to speak to you yet either. Don't want to get you down or anything, but at tea tonight, I noticed he'd scrawled out "BEST" on that "WORLD'S BEST DAD" mug we all got you for your birthday years ago, and scribbled "WORST" above it. Sorry – like I say, I don't want to make you feel bad, but I'm just trying to explain why it might not be a good idea to call the house for a couple of days.

You could always call me on my mobile or email me, if you want.

That would be nice.
Please.
Love
Heather x

## The Loving Them Button

Beans.

Beans, beans, stupid, minging old beans. If I had beans-on-stupid-minging-toast for tea for one more night, I might turn into a bright orange, deranged beany freak.

It was no wonder that when Becca's mum and dad asked me to stay for tea, I said "YESSS!!" very loudly, before they got to the end of their sentence.

Anyway, it was Wednesday (i.e., nine days after The Bombshell), and I'd gone round to do my homework at Becca's 'cause a) that's what I often did, and b) the atmosphere at Becca's house was way better than mine. Mainly because her dad hadn't just left without a proper explanation, her mum wasn't hibernating in bed, she didn't have a younger sister who was morphing into a gremlin, and she didn't have a tea-time diet that consisted entirely of big-brother-cooked beans on stupid, minging toast. . .

"It must be very hard for your poor mother. And you, Heather, dear," said Mrs Fitzgerald, as she ladled a huge portion of homemade fish pie on to my plate.

"*Very* hard," Mr Fitzgerald muttered, like a sympathetic echo to his wife.

"It's OK," I lied.

*Boy*, was I getting good at lying recently.

"How's your mum? Is she still ill?" Mum's friend (and boss) Lorraine had said when she called last night.

"Yes, she's still got laryngitis," I fibbed, not quite able to tell Lorraine the truth, though I couldn't figure out why.

"Is everything all right at home?" asked Tallie's teacher, Miss de Rossi, when I picked my sister up today.

"Yes," I fibbed. "Why?"

"Oh, nothing in particular," Miss de Rossi had said, watching in slight bewilderment as Tallie stomped around the classroom wearing most of the dressing-up box at once, and loudly banging some cymbals. "She's just been a lot more . . . *exuberant* lately."

Exuberant. I guess that was a good way to describe a little girl who until recently liked to co-ordinate her hair bobbles to her tights and came home with "Best Behaved In Class!" awards on a regular basis.

"Broccoli?"

Mrs Fitzgerald was hovering over my plate, ready to drop a steamy, buttery pile of greenery on to my plate.

Green, not beany orange. Mmm. . .

The smell of hot apple pie drifted through from the kitchen.

Y'know, Mr and Mrs Fitzgerald had always been what you might call *pleasant* to me, but I always got the feeling that in their eyes, I was a bit of a default friend for Becca. I think they'd have preferred her to have a friend as pretty and as groomed and sensible as she was, instead of me and my untameable hair and school shirts that looked permanently rumpled from the minute I put them on and stupid obsessions with stupid song titles or the history of soup or whatever I was into that week.

But today, they seemed genuinely warm and friendly. Plus they had real food in their house *and* apple pie for pudding.

"Yes, please." I nodded hungrily at the broccoli, and wondered if Becca's parents might consider fostering me.

I wasn't just fed-up of eating Jo-Jo's one-trick teas, I was also suddenly very tired of being in sole charge of the washing (clothes and dishes and kid sisters), and having to be the Fashion Police every morning, as Tallie tried to leave the house in more and more bizarre outfits and hairdos.

In that mad second, I decided I really wouldn't mind leaving my lovely but cluttered room and sleeping on a blow-up bed on the floor of Becca's mauve-tinted bedroom, in the Fitzgerald's nice and normal house. I'd love to go into a bathroom in the morning and not fret that the toothpaste/shampoo/loo roll had run out. I'd love not to have to go into a darkened bedroom and ask Mum if she wanted anything to eat, when I knew the answer would be no. I'd love not to dread answering the phone, in case it was friends of the family that I'd have to lie to, all because I was too ashamed to tell the truth, or too loyal, or something else that I hadn't figured out yet.

Wow, I ached for some boring, uncomplicated normality. . .

"But it must be difficult, not having your dad around," Mrs Fitzgerald continued, putting down the bowl of broccoli and cutting into a big, crusty loaf of bread.

"You know, Mrs Samson the science teacher is leaving at the end of term!" Becca suddenly chipped in, very brightly.

Bless her, she was trying to change the subject, in a madly clunky way. (Becca's exceptionally good at most things, with the exception of being subtle.)

The thing was, I wasn't exactly sure *why* she was trying to change the subject; after all, I *had* said she could tell her parents about what had happened at home, seeing as she was (of course) my best friend.

I'd just asked her not to tell them *everything*, if you see what I mean. Not the stuff about Tallie turning into a gremlin, and Jo-Jo pretending Dad had evaporated off the face of the planet, and specially not about Mum hiding out under the duvet.

"She's leaving your school? Well, *that's* interesting," said Mrs Fitzgerald with a vague, disinterested nod in Becca's direction. "But anyway, Heather, has your dad been in touch much?"

"Um, no, not really," I replied, nibbling at a forkful of fish pie. Since his call on Monday, all I'd had was a quick email saying he was a bit gutted to hear about the "WORLD'S WORST DAD" message, but that he understood everyone needed a bit of time and space. (Yeah, time and space. I think Jo-Jo might need three millennia and to know Dad was living in a different galaxy before he was ready to forgive him.)

"I hope all the upset doesn't affect Jo-Jo's studies too much," Mr Fitzgerald muttered, shaking his head. "It'll be exam time for him soon, I suppose. Though for a young man of his age, it's completely understandable that he'd feel so hostile towards your dad and protective of all of you. It's really unforgivable of your father."

I glanced over at Becca.

*Er, how much HAS she told her parents exactly?* I suddenly wondered.

Becca's long brown fringe was masking her eyes from this angle, but she seemed to be hyper-interested in her fish pie all of a sudden.

"And your poor mum – she must be worried about the effect it's all having on little Tallie. But of course, she probably doesn't realize, what with her taking to her bed."

Becca glanced up from her tea and gave me a pink-cheeked, pursed-lips smile that I think was meant to be a silent way of saying, "sorry".

I gave her the tiniest, practically invisible-to-the-human-eye shrug, the sort only a best friend could pick up on. And Becca *was* my best friend; whenever I'd felt down this last week or so she'd kept singing (or sometimes texting, when we were in class) that "Things Can Only Get Better" song off the CD I gave her.

Like I said, Becca's only problem was that whole can't-get-the-hang-of-being-subtle thing. A specific problem with that was – apart from being very silent about her unspoken lurve for my brother – she couldn't stop her mouth working at the same time as her brain was thinking.

Which, when you think about it, can be a very dangerous thing. . .

"I don't know how he could do it," tutted Mr Fitzgerald thoughtfully. "Not to a lovely woman like your mother. And to walk out on his family like that. . ."

I felt a quiver of rage. It was all right for *me* to think that way about my dad, but I suddenly wasn't sure I liked to hear other people bad-mouthing him.

"Y'know, Miss Samson's got a job at St Aidan's School!" Becca tried her rubbish distraction technique again, but it was too late, and too lame.

Suddenly, I'd lost my appetite. . .

Home, sweet(ish) home.

A home that was thankfully quiet, with no one around to ask me nosey questions.

I was still slightly rattled about my tea-time grilling from Becca's parents. Maybe I was being over-sensitive, but by the end it got to feel more like they were fishing for gossip about my dad rather than just being sympathetic. Now I'd had time to think about it on the way home, I realized it was probably a bit of *both*.

Still, Mr and Mrs Fitzgerald's conversation-turned-inquisition had caused some serious brain overload, and my poor brain was *already* ping-ponging with way too many clashing thoughts about my family situation, thank you very much. Take Mum, for example: my normally pretty, chatty, friendly mum. I was totally on her side over what had happened, of course. But I was also totally freaked about her retreating into her bedroom like *it* was a cave, and *she* was a monk taking a ten-year vow of silence. And by the way, I mean freaked as in worried, AND freaked as in mortified.

And then there was Dad, who I should hate . . . but couldn't. Even when someone does something that makes you miserable, how do you switch off your Loving Them Button, just like that? Anger had made Jo-Jo manage, I guess. And Tallie? Well, she was only five, and cross and confused, and probably just had her Love Button switched to pause.

Dad. . .

I glanced up at the coat rack, and wished his brown jacket was still there. I wished he was around to nag us about brushing our teeth every five seconds. I wished I could flip open the *British Hit Singles and Albums* book and try to test him on songs in the charts back when he was young and groovy (Dad always seemed a tiny bit less bewildered by my stupid interests than the rest of my family). I just wished he was here, really.

But he wasn't, and neither was anyone else, by the sound (or no sound) of it. Not downstairs, anyway. It was past eight o'clock, so Tallie would've been in bed by now, ditto Mum (of course). And Jo-Jo? I must have just missed him. Otherwise he'd be poured along one of the sofas, lost in his i-Pod and a music magazine. Well, it was Wednesday . . . his usual night for school squash club. He hadn't gone last week (life too weird), but after giving Tallie her tea (mmm, beans), maybe he'd decided to pack his racquet and get back in the swing of things (ha-ha, spot the pun). He was probably on a court right now, imagining the little black ball was Dad's head.

Wandering aimlessly through to the kitchen, I glanced at the dried-bean-stained plates in the sink, then padded through to the living room and checked out a still-wet painting laid out on the coffee table, that Tallie must have been busy doing before bedtime. It looked like a . . . a Halloween rainbow. Arcs of orange and black swirled across the white paper with – oops! – semi-congealed dribbles of colour plopped on to the cream carpet. (Shopping list for tomorrow: carpet cleaner.)

Side-stepping the dribbles, I went to sit down on the sofa, thinking at first that I might stick on the telly and let some bland soap or stupid police show soothe my frazzled brain. But I wasn't in the mood. After having a muse while rocking on the spot, I decided that the only thing I half-fancied doing was retreating to my room and digging out my scrapbooks of *Far Side* cartoons. Stupid jokes about monsters who are scared of kids and cows who liked to party was my only hope of vaguely cheering up.

But first, I needed to peek. . .

"Mum?" I said, in a small, slightly wobbly voice.

No answer in the darkness – she was sleeping. But the light from the hallway gave out just enough of a glow for me to make out the box of tissues on the bed (the crumpled used ones would be just out of sight on the floor), the pile of squashy soft toys (Tallie was depositing them with her, one by one), the glint of the glass vase (filled with flowers by Krystyna when she was here on Monday), and the gentle up and down movement of the duvet as Mum breathed (phew, she wasn't dead).

Next, it was time to peek in at Tallie. Except . . . except my attention was grabbed by the soft light spilling out of Jo-Jo's room, and the tinny sound of some radio track rattling in the background.

"Jo-Jo?" I said tentatively, tapping my bitten nails at my brother's bedroom door as I pushed it open. "Oh. . .!"

The girl sitting on the bed was a total stranger.

The girl sitting on the bed looked about nineteen or twenty.

The girl sitting on the bed had the palest of blue eyes, staring out of two smudgy rings of black eyeshadow.

The girl sitting on the bed was a black-and-purple wearing, curiously-pierced goth.

The girl sitting on the bed said, "Jo-Jo's out – he'll be back later."

Totally stumped about what to say or do, I reverted to being the big moose I always was in times of stress.

"You're not a burglar, are you?" I asked her.

Like yeah, the criminal world is chock full of goth girl burglars. Specially goth girl burglars who happen to know my brother's name and whereabouts.

"No, I'm not," said the girl.

Without saying another dumb word, I closed the door softly.

For the sake of my sanity, it was time to run away and lie down in a quiet, darkened room.

Or in *my* case, a cluttered, messy one, with the streetlight beaming in through the Velux blind I'd managed to break a while back. (So don't expect to hear anything sane coming from me anytime soon. . .)

**From:**    **wombat**

**Subject:**  **Well, hello**

**Date:**    **Wednesday 4 April**

**To:**      **rsmith@smiledentalgroup**


Hi Dad

I tried to go to sleep early, but couldn't. So I switched on my computer and was v. chuffed to see your email. Glad you've had a chance now to listen to the CD I made for you. Did you listen to that in the car, or wherever you're staying? Maybe I can come there sometime. . .

Everything is OK here. Well, OK-ish. Tallie is turning into a feral cat – found her asleep in the corner of her room half an hour ago, in a nest of duvet. When I picked her up and moved her back on to the bed, I swear she hissed at me in her sleep.

Got to go (going to read song-title lists at the back of the *British Hit Singles and Albums* book till I feel sleepy).

Email me again soon.

Or call.

Or something.

Love

Heather x

**From:** wombat

**Subject:** Me again

**Date:** Wednesday 4 April

**To:** rsmith@smiledentalgroup

Hi Dad

Got to the "B" section of the *British Hit Singles and Albums* book and saw there was a song called "Being Boiled" (by the Human League). Now I can't sleep for dreaming about being chased down the street in my pyjamas by a giant boiled egg.
   Is that what they call an anxiety dream?
   Love
   Heather x

# The mystery goth

The wombat nickname: I got that (briefly) in Year Six, when the class torturer, Paulo Coia, caught sight of my school photo.

I have to say I didn't look my gorgeous best.

I had a sort of pudding-bowl haircut that Mum had tried to glue into position with hairspray before I left the house in the morning. But a day of standard walking around and sitting in class was enough for my hair to ping up rebelliously. In the photo, I'm trying to smile but failing, knowing that Mum and Dad are going to have a mantelpiece weighed down with school photos of Jo-Jo looking like a fledgling indie band member, Tallie looking like the child star of a particularly cute washing powder commercial, and one of me looking like a wombat, as Paulo Coia so kindly pointed out.

He only said it out of frustration, 'cause I wouldn't tell him what the "P" in Heather "P" Smith stood for, but he was sort of right. Sadly, I *could* see the resemblance between the self-consciously smirking me and a small, pudgy animal that looks like a cross between a dog and a hamster.

Luckily, the wombat tag only stuck in *my* head; no one else heard Paulo's comments, and he moved to Bolton for Year Seven, where he could tease and torture a whole new bunch of people.

Brushing my teeth in the mirror now, after a decent night's sleep (except for the mad boiled-egg dreams), I had to admit I didn't seem remotely like a wombat any more. Maybe a meerkat, with a wig on. From Year Six to Year Eight, I'd changed quite a lot, from small and round to long and lanky. And the pudding-bowl haircut was now a non-style that was *meant* to be the same as Becca's past-the-shoulders, swooping-long-fringe look, but turned out more like a shaggy shire horse on a windy day.

Still, even though I realized that I looked more like a cross between a windswept shire horse and a meerkat, I did feel a tiny bit less *mad* today. Maybe it was just the fact that I'd slept for ten hours solid (better than the snap-shot snoozes I'd been having for the last week and a half), but I had this faint little glimmer of hope that things were maybe starting to get back to normal-ish. Nothing major had happened; I mean, Mum hadn't sprung out of bed tra-la-la-ing, and Dad hadn't turned up with roses and apologies and promises to move back in. It was just a couple of small but somehow reassuring somethings, like the fact that I'd found Tallie playing her old favourite, doll's tea party, on the living-room floor just now. And Jo-Jo going back to his squash club last night was a good si—

Hold it.

Hold it *right* there.

My deep sleep might have temporarily wiped certain chunks of my memory, but now it all came flooding back big-time: the fact that there was a mystery goth sitting on the edge of my brother's bed last night. A mystery goth who'd left her bat-shaped hair clips here on the glass bathroom shelf, in between Tallie's strawberry-flavour toothpaste and Mum's silver contact lens case.

*How come Jo-Jo's friend forgot them last night?* I wondered to myself, reaching out and picking one up. A few strands of long black (and purple) hairs trailed over the top of the hot tap as I turned the beaded black bat over in my fingers.

Hey.

Let's think about this.

Q: Why would people take hair clips out?

- The preferable answer: They're changing their hairstyle. (The mystery goth might have fiddled with her 'do prior to leaving last night.)
- The possible answer: They're about to jump in the shower or bath. (I did a double-take in the mirror – only me and my horsey reflection here in the room.)
- The deeply unpleasant answer: They're going to bed. (Omigod – did the mystery goth stay the night in my brother's *room*?!!).

"*Heatherrrr!!*" came a sudden shout from somewhere downstairs. "Can I have some breakfast, please?"

Tallie.

Trying to spit thoughts of unexpected overnight guests out of my mouth along with toothpaste foam, I realized my first priority was to get Tallie fed and watered for school, before getting to my second priority, i.e., taking a tray of breakfast to Mum, in the vague hope she'd eat something, and not just survive on thin air and misery.

Thudding downstairs, I set to it.

Flick the radio to something loud and dancey, stick the kettle on, bung teabag in cup, grab bowls of cereal for me, Tallie and Mum. Now to get the orange juice and milk out of the fridge.

I yanked the handle and . . . stopped dead. The chill of the fridge misted out on my face, as I stared at the unexpected contents of the cheese compartment. OK, so we hadn't had any actual cheese in there for a few days (something else on my shopping list), but I hadn't expected to see four bottles of black, purple, dark green and blood-red nail varnish in place of a slab of farmhouse Cheddar.

What the goth was going on?!

"Tallie. . ." I called out, closing the fridge door and heading through to the living room.

"Is breakfast ready?" she asked hopefully, glancing up from her tea party.

Uh-oh. I hadn't looked too closely at the dolls till now. They had some very interesting face art going on, courtesy of a pack of felt pens by the side of Tallie's pink, fluffy bunny slippers. Baby Annabell in particular looked like she'd been attacked by a deranged tattoo artist. No baby – even a plastic one – deserved to have a spiderweb scrawled across the top of its bald pink head.

"Um, no," I replied, struggling to drag my eyes from the disconcerting sight of Ballerina Barbie with a completely blue face. Good grief, Tallie was the girl who used to use a pretend iron on her dolls' clothes on a twice-weekly basis. She was the kid who had to polish her Disney Princess tiara before every wearing.

"But my tummy is rumbly and grumbly," Tallie smiled charmingly at me.

"Sure, but I just wanted to ask you something. Have you seen a strange girl in Jo-Jo's room this morning?"

I dropped my voice, in case strange girls or Jo-Jo overheard me.

"No," said Tallie, pouring out a fake cup of tea for Blue-faced Barbie.

"What about last night? Did you meet a friend – like a freaky-looking girl friend – of Jo-Jo's before you went to bed?"

"No," said Tallie, wrapped up in her polite game with her vandalized guests.

OK, so it was just me reading too much into a couple of hair clips. And, er, a cheese box full of nail varnishes. There could be a simple (but surreal) explanation for those, couldn't there? After all, Tallie's hairbrush had found its way in there the other day. Maybe the nail varnishes in the fridge had something to do with an art project Jo-Jo was doing at school or something.

One problem with that: Jo-Jo didn't *do* art as one of his sixth-form subjects. . .

"I'll get breakfast," I muttered, turning and hurrying towards the kitchen.

Tallie's soft voice muttered something in return.

"What?" I asked, spinning round, and expecting to

hear a request for pink milk or a sploosh of honey on her cereal.

"I saw her suitcase, though. It's *really* big."

The glass living-room door gently swung closed, right in my totally stunned face. . .

**Subject:  Surprise surprise**

**Date:     Thursday 5 April**

**To:        rsmith@smiledentalgroup**


Hi Dad

Guess what? Jo-Jo's got a room-mate. We haven't been formally introduced yet, but I did just pass the bathroom and heard them in there chatting and laughing, above the sound of the shower.

I think she (yes, *she*) must be staying a while – I just took a peek at her suitcase and it's the size of a small lorry.

Everything's getting a bit surreal round here.

Got to go – will be late getting Tallie to school.

Love

Heather x

# Exceptionally non-normal times

Did you know there are 2,200 bubbles in one Aero chocolate bar?

I have a talent for knowing stupid but interesting facts like that. I know *lots* of stupid but interesting facts, in fact. (Did you know that polar bears have black skin? Or that you have over eight metres of intestine?) Last year, I went through a phase of collecting books with titles like *101 Things You Didn't Know That You Didn't Know*, which are packed to the brim with stupid but interesting facts.

It's just that I find it quite soothing to think of stupid but interesting facts when you don't want your brain to wander into the dangerous area of unsettling stuff.

Unsettling stuff like your supposedly smart, well-behaved seventeen-year-old brother moving his older, weirder girlfriend into his room without asking anyone. As if it's perfectly OK to do that. Or maybe he thought Mum and me and Tallie wouldn't notice or something. (Yeah, like you're *really* going to miss a goth lurking around your house, leaving her bat hair clips in the bathroom and her nail varnish in the cheese compartment.)

So today after school, I picked up Tallie, and spent the walk home telling her stupid facts ("Did you know that prehistoric penguins were six-feet tall?") instead of dwelling on the uncomfortable subject of our overnight visitor.

Oh, I am such a coward, I really am.

This morning, I should have knocked on the bathroom door as soon as I heard the laughing and chit-chatting, and straight out asked Jo-Jo who his friend was. That's what I *should've* done, considering I've known Jo-Jo for ooh, the whole of my thirteen-year-old life, and got on pretty well with him.

Instead, I ran past the bathroom, pretending I couldn't hear the chatting and giggling going on inside, dropped Mum's tray off to her, then after a kiss on her sleeping cheek, I zipped into my room and rattled off a quick, moany email to Dad. Next, I'd hurtled downstairs, scooped out a bunch of clean-but-crushed clothes from the tumble dryer, flung them on Tallie, and hurtled out the door with her, without a backwards "bye" to my brother.

It was as if there was another elephant, in another corner, all over again, only *this* elephant was goth-shaped, rather than Dad-shaped. Soon, we wouldn't be able to *move* in our house for tripping over elephants. . .

"I'll get it!" yelped Tallie, hurtling ahead of me as we got through the front door, same as she had done all the way home from her school.

"Hello?" she chirruped, once she'd grabbed the ringing phone,

Meanwhile, I glanced nervously up the stairs, wondering if the mystery goth and her really big suitcase were still here.

Maybe I should go check the cheese compartment. . .

"S'for you!!" said Tallie, holding the receiver out towards me.

I stretched out to grab it from her, automatically assuming it was Becca, phoning to sing "Things Can Only Get Better", or witter about something she'd forgotten to witter about at school earlier.

"Tallie! Tallie!! TALLIE!!!"

Huh?

Had Becca developed a very strange throat virus since I last saw her, twenty minutes ago? It's just that I didn't remember Becca having a man's voice. Specially one that sounded exactly like my dad's . . .

"Dad?"

"Heather? Where's Tallie gone to? She went quiet as soon as I said it was me, and started to ask how she was!"

At first, I thought he sounded grumpy, but almost straight away, I realized it was more like hurt and confused.

Tallie, on the other hand, was skipping up the stairs, singing, "Twinkle, Twinkle, chocolate bar! My dad drives a rusty old car. . .!", and not sounding sad or confused at all. Though I knew she *had* to be feeling that way, or she wouldn't have deliberately ignored Dad just now. It was like Jo-Jo pretending Dad was a figment of someone else's imagination, or me, being nice to Dad in my emails, even though I still wanted to yell at him now for not telling us where he was.

I guess that in exceptionally non-normal times, people act in non-normal ways. . .

"Listen – I got your email about this – this *person* Jo-Jo's got staying. What's your brother playing at? And why hasn't your mum put her foot down?!" Now Dad really *did* sound grumpy.

"I . . . I don't know if Mum knows," I said, breaking out in a cold sweat.

I'd badly wanted to blurt to Dad in my email this morning, but now I sort of wished I hadn't.

"How could your mum not know?" Dad demanded, sounding exasperated.

"She's . . . she's had this really bad migraine thing, and she's been in bed," I said, rubbing and scratching at my nose.

(Lying was getting worryingly easy.)

"Oh. Is she OK?"

"Yeah."

(Oops, another lie. Silly me.)

"Well, get Jo-Jo – *I'll* talk to him."

In some strange twist of synchronicity, a blast of something loud and guitar-based blasted from upstairs.

I pressed the receiver closer to my head, in the hope of drowning out any giveaway sounds.

"He's not home from school yet," I lied, lied, lied.

I heard Dad give a long, low sigh, that started grumpy but ended up sounding hurt and confused again, all in one breath.

"Right, right. Wish I could come round and get this sorted out, but I suppose it's all too soon. . ."

He could say *that* again. There wouldn't be a "Welcome home!" banner outside, ready to greet him – not if Jo-Jo had anything to do with it.

"Listen," said Dad, suddenly sounding slightly brighter. "Why don't you and I meet up for a coffee soon, Heather, and you can properly fill me in with what's going on at home? Yeah?"

"Yes!!" I answered eagerly, like I'd just been offered an envelope with a thousand pounds in it, no strings attached.

But of course there *were* strings attached to meeting Dad for coffee, strings like the uncomfortable truth about Mum's hibernation. And how Mum (and Jo-Jo and Tallie) might feel about me meeting up with our traitor dad.

To tell or not to tell, that was the question. . .

"Look, I'll have a think about times and places, and get back to you by email. All right?"

"Course!"

OK, so I had a bit of time to fester over the to-tell-or-not-to-tell problem. But the worry ulcer would be worth it, just to see Dad.

I felt a sharp tug at my heart as he said "bye". Just like last night, I had another, sudden bad case of missing him.

"Heather?"

Mum!

Another tug at my heart, hearing Mum's voice call down to me. I'd missed her too – I hadn't heard her voice as anything more than a deflated whisper for way more than a week. Her voice, fairly clear and loud just now, was one of the nicest sounds I'd ever heard. . .

"Hi!" I said, swinging by the doorpost into what I guess we'd now have to stop referring to as "Mum and Dad's room". "How're you doing?"

I was out of breath, from hurtling up the stairs practically six at a time.

It was easy to see how she was doing: better. I mean, not *great* – she was as pale and drawn as some consumptive heroine in a Charles Dickens' novel. All she needed was a frilly, white cotton nightie and a lace-edged hankie speckled lightly with blood and she'd be a dead cert for a major part in the next TV adaptation of *Bleak House* or whatever.

"I'm OK," she said, sitting up in bed, propped against her pillows, with the most fabulous of small smiles.

Tallie was curled up like a cat by her side, shoes kicked off, busy with something that I couldn't quite make out with only the mauve-shaded bedside light on.

"All the better for seeing my girls!" Mum added happily, giving Tallie a cuddle.

I thought about asking if she minded me opening the curtains and letting some sky blast in, and then I thought, *nah* – just do it.

After some major wincing (hey, daylight hadn't got a look in here in the last ten days), Mum smiled and spoke some more.

"How's Becca?"

Huh? Mum comes out of self-imposed exile and wants to know about my best friend? That was very sweet and everything, but kind of *weird* under the circumstances.

"She's, uh, good," I replied, moving aside some of the pile of soft toys Tallie had strewn on the bed and making space for myself.

"Tallie was saying you were on the phone to her just now."

So, I wasn't the *only* liar, liar, pants on fire in this house.

"Mmm," I mumbled, glancing at my little sis, who was handing something to Mum.

"Here. A present!"

It was a star, a wibbly-wobbly star cut out of paper, using special wibbly-wobbly-edged scissors. How sweet. What a typical five-year-old present it was, except for the fact that Tallie had cut her wibbly-wobbly star out of the pages of an old *Maisie* book. And Mum didn't seem the slightest bit bothered. (Excuse me, but didn't Mum drum into us all the importance of bookmarks, and the evil of spoiling books by folding corners of pages over?)

"Oh, thank you, darling!" Mum beamed. "That's just like a pendant I used to wear. . . Heather can you get my jewellery box over?"

Mum's antique, sage-green jewellery box was full of intriguing layers of tiny boxed-off sections, with individual earrings and necklaces and beautiful polished and beaded things nestled like precious birds' eggs, each in their perfectly fitting place.

Growing up, it was an understood no-go area. Now and again, the box and its treasure was opened up and revealed to me and Tallie, and we gazed on it with strict no-touching wonder.

But what was I saying before about non-normal behaviour in non-normal times?

"Here!" said Mum, pulling out a titanium-coloured star pendant, and draping it over Tallie's head.

Two minutes later, and the three of us were wearing the entire contents of the box, in a spectacular and stunning fashion. It was a game of dress-up bling.

"I don't remember this. . ." I said, lifting a heavy hand weighed down with a variety of lovely but mismatching bangles, bracelets and rings.

I was wiggling my "wedding" finger, showing off a gold ring with a cream-coloured pearl in the middle.

Mum leant forward, sending a looky-likey tiara (a necklace of amber stones that Tallie had balanced on her head) slithering off on to the duvet.

"Ah, that was my grandmother's. Her engagement ring. A pearl for a Pearl," said Mum, her head suddenly full of warm thoughts of a gran – our great-gran – that we'd never met.

I'd heard of Pearl, of course. She'd have been ninety-six by now, if she hadn't gone and died of dancing (another story, for another day) a week after I was born, and the day before Mum and Dad went to the council offices to formally register my name. In a flurry of fondness, my parents ditched their original plans to call me Heather (who knows why) Ella (pretty and kind of cool) Smith, and opted for Heather *Pearl* Smith at the last moment.

Pearl.

What kind of old-fashioned, fanciful name is that for a teenage girl in the twenty-first century? "Heather" hardly suited me, so how could I live with "Pearl"? Here's the dictionary definition of "pearl": *A smooth, lustrous gem*. No one – not even the people who loved me best – could ever describe me as smooth (make that clunky), lustrous (scruffy) or a gem (*germy*, maybe – I get a lot of colds, remember).

No, it was better that Pearl hid away as just "P" in my name, and at least gave me a bit of pleasure by using it to frustrate the likes of Paulo Coia. . .

"I guess that was thoughtful," I said, studying the obviously old ring. "Your granddad giving her an engagement ring with a stone that matched her name."

"Oh, she didn't get it from *him*," laughed Mum. "She got it from another boyfriend. But she always wore this one as well as the one my grandad gave her –"

Mum held up Tallie's left thumb, where a green-chipped ring glinted.

"– because she liked it so much. Not that my grandad approved. But you know what Pearl was like!"

Well, no I didn't, not really. I mean, I knew a handful of facts, like you do about anyone in your family that lived forever ago. I knew that she was little during the First World War, worked in a parachute-making factory in the Second World War, was addicted to entering competitions in newspapers, and died of dancing (like I say, that's quite another story).

"Hey! I *thought* I heard you laughing!" said Jo-Jo, appearing at the door, doing his overarm stretch, like he hadn't a care in the world, or a girl hidden in his room. "You look ridiculous!"

"Thanks, honey!" Mum grinned, her face lighting up as she started to take off her strands of beads.

"No – don't do that! Leave all that stuff on!" said Jo-Jo, ginning back at her. "I meant ridiculous in a *good* way!"

"*Is* there such a thing?" asked Mum, raising her eyes at him, but leaving her necklaces where they were.

"Course there is!" said Jo-Jo, before turning away from us for a second (with his arm stretched up like that, he looked like he was doing the next step in a complicated yoga stretch). "Hey! Hey, Sylv!"

What?

*What* was he shouting?

"Sylv! Come here and meet my mum!" he yelled, taking a few steps back into the hall so that whoever was called "Sylv" could hear him above the Green Day album that was booming out from his room.

Omigod. This could set Mum back – she'd only just perked up and now Jo-Jo was going to flaunt his stay-over, much older goth girlfriend.

I had to give her a bit of warning. . .

"Mum – there was a girl in Jo-Jo's room last n—"

"It's all right," she said, patting my hand and making her bangles jangle. "I know."

I glanced at Tallie, who looked up, wide-eyed, from her careful vandalizing of the *Maisie* book. She was as stumped as me, it seemed.

"Jo-Jo," Mum called out to him. "Can you explain to the girls, please?"

Eek! Here came a waft of black and purple, swirling out from my brother's room, and heading towards us, and in particular Mum in her sickbed, like some terrifying vampire-ess. . .

"Hello," said the vampire-ess, in a high, girlish voice.

She had a hole in the toe of her black and purple

stripy tights, I noticed. I also noticed she was trying to hide it by nudging that foot under her other one.

OK, so maybe she wasn't so terrifying. She actually looked a little bit terrified herself, now that I could see her in the light of day. She was blinking a lot, which I supposed was a sign of nerves, but I guess could've been an allergic reaction to her heavy, smoky eye make-up.

The way she was anxiously twirling the silver necklace at her neck – some sort of broken heart shape – now that really *did* look like an anxious tic, just like my dumb nose scratching.

"Hello, Sylv, pleased to meet you," said Mum graciously, even though she – actually *all* of us – must have looked a proper sight, in the dress-up bling. "I'm Joanna, and this is Heather and Tallulah."

"Hi," said the girl called Sylv, waving a black-varnished, nail-bitten hand at us.

"Sylv's my mate," said Jo-Jo, doing what Mum had asked and beginning his explanation, before eyeballing me specifically and adding, "and *only* a mate."

I didn't know if I really believed that. I'd never heard him talking about a "Sylv" before. And why *should* I believe it, if Jo-Jo didn't believe Dad saying he hadn't left us for anyone?

"Sylv's had hassles at home, so she's staying for a while, till she gets herself sorted. Mum's OK with that, aren't you, Mum?"

"Yes, like I said last night, it's fine," said Mum, leaning back against the pillow and wilting a little, as if all this talking and glamming-up and formal introductions had tired her out. She (and Dad) would never have allowed a girl mate to stay over in his room before (before The Bombshell). I hoped my brother hadn't just taken advantage of our mother while she had the energy of a particularly soggy lettuce leaf.

"Here! A present!" trilled Tallie, suddenly kneeing her way across a myriad of soft toys and handing the goth girl another wibbly-wobbly star.

"Um, thanks," said Sylv warily, glancing at the three bespangled female members of Jo-Jo's family on the toy-covered bed.

She probably wondered if she'd accidentally blundered into a bizarre, parallel universe, instead of a four-bed semi in the suburbs. Which is exactly how *I* felt.

Hey, maybe I had more in common with Sylv the strange goth than I realized. . .

From:      **wombat**

Subject:   **When will I see you again?***

Date:      **Thursday 5 April**

To:        **rsmith@smiledentalgroup**


Hi Dad

Really looking forward to seeing you soon. Really, really.

I can tell you some stuff about Jo-Jo's friend now, though. Her name is Sylv, and she's staying for a few days 'cause of some problem at home. Mum is OK with it. Sylv seems very quiet. She has her nails painted black, and has three piercings (that I can see): one in her nose, one in her eyebrow, and one in her auricle! I know – weird, huh? I'll have to ask her if it hurts, like a *lot*. If she ever speaks before she moves out, I mean. And if she does speak, I've got to ask her why she put her nail varnish in the fridge. Though I'm not really sure if I *want* her to speak to me.

By the way, did you know this strange but interesting fact? The first recorded people to wear nail varnish were the Chinese royal family in 3,000 BC. I don't know where they kept theirs, but you can bet it wasn't a cheese compartment.


* According to the *British Book of Hit Singles and Albums*, a Number One for The Three Degrees in 1974, when you were just five, Dad!

Like I say, really, really looking forward to seeing you. A lot.
Love
Heather x

# The grand scheme of things

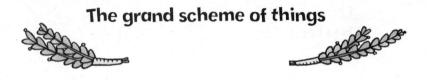

I knew Sylv chatted, 'cause I heard her talking (and laughing) with Jo-Jo in his room all the time. And I'd heard her chatting to Mum in her room too. I'd even heard her chatting to Tallie, telling her that the auricle piercing had hurt like crazy (well, now I knew), and that no, girls of five couldn't get it done. And no, "Sylv" wasn't short for "silver".

The one person Sylv didn't talk to was *me*.

"Maybe it's because you haven't talked to *her*?" suggested Becca

It was Monday, the first day of two weeks' worth of Easter holidays, and we'd been hanging out at the park all day. Now we were ambling towards my house, with Tallie zooming along in front of us on Jo-Jo's old scooter that she'd hauled out of the shed. (Poor Blue-faced Barbie was being dragged by a string alongside the scooter, her blue head bouncing along the pavement, now that Tallie had decided the doll was *Doggy* Barbie, i.e., the closest our family had ever got to a pet, apart from *me*.)

That stuff that Becca had just said, about me not talking to Sylv – I knew it was true, I really did, but didn't want to admit that obvious thought to myself, 'cause then it would seem like *I* was the one in the wrong, and not the invading goth, who was no nearer moving out, after five nights so far.

But I still didn't plan on talking to her.

I guess it was 'cause I'd been hoping-against-hope for things to start feeling even the tiniest bit more normal, and with Jo-Jo going and moving a goth stranger into the house, I felt like he'd pushed that nice, longed-for normal feeling even further away.

Anyway, who was *I* kidding?

My family was nowhere near normal, not even *vaguely*.

Mum was chirpier, and eating, and even had a radio in her room now, but she still hadn't left her bed.

And get this: the moment school was out, Jo-Jo began to wear eyeliner on the inside of his bottom eyelids. Lucky it was the start of the holidays, or he'd be banned, banned, banned.

Tallie had borrowed some from him (or from Sylv?) and done the same thing to herself and all her dolls, and terrified the woman on the check-out in Tesco when I went shopping with her at the weekend. The woman had been all ready to coo, till she got a good look at the junior goth princess and her panda eyes, and instantly shuddered instead.

I hadn't been able to persuade Tallie to take the eyeliner off before we went out that day, and after my little sis wailing the house down, Mum had acted like an over-exhausted referee and told me it didn't matter, "in the grand scheme of things".

Well, I wasn't sure about the "grand scheme of things", but I knew I hadn't found it a whole heap of fun in the supermarket, either at the check-out, *or* when Tallie had stared at the kid on the Postman Pat kiddie ride outside and scared him off, screaming, into the arms of his dad. . .

"Still, you've got to talk to her *some* time. You have to ask about the nail varnish in the fridge!" Becca pointed out, as the three of us (*four*, if you counted Doggy Barbie) walked up the path to my house.

"I don't need to know *that* badly!" I said with a careless shrug.

"Well, *I* could ask her!"

"Don't you dare!" I warned Becca, as I put the key in the door. Choosing not to speak to Sylv was the only tiny chunk of control I had in my life at the moment, and I didn't want my best friend to go and blow it for me. "Promise!"

"I promise!"

Still, I understood her curiosity. A girl with a secret passion can't be expected not to come and nosey at the girl who's sharing that secret passion's room, can she?

"My doggy needs food," announced Tallie, diving between our legs and running towards the kitchen.

I was about to follow her inside when a heard a very unexpected noise.

"Hold it!" I said suddenly, pausing in the front doorway.

"What's up?" asked Becca, craning her neck to see over my shoulder.

She was probably panicking that I could hear the sound of snogging going on. I'd already told her (and watched her try to hide her shock) that I wasn't sure about Jo-Jo's claims about Sylv being just a mate.

But the sound I heard was *much* more surprising than the slurp of a snog.

"It's Mum. *Mum's* voice. . ." I muttered.

"Yeah, so?" said Becca. "She lives here!"

"She hasn't lived *downstairs* for two weeks," I pointed out, going from nought to sixty as I strode at high speed along the corridor into the living room. I finally saw her – dressed, showered, blonde hair scraped back in a neat, stubby ponytail – sitting having a cup of tea and biscuits in the conservatory, and lost in conversation with Krystyna.

"Hi, Mum!" I said, getting closer, and giving Krystyna a shy smile.

*She* must have done the tea and biscuits. She maybe even shoved Mum under the shower for all I knew.

"Heather! Hi, honey!" Mum beamed at me.

Oh, *wow*, this was good. Some kind of miracle had happened while we were all at the park. Maybe Krystyna had flicked a magic duster over Mum and glittered her back to life.

I had no idea what Mum normally paid Krystyna, but I felt like immediately demanding an instant pay rise for her.

"You look nice!" I said uselessly, giving her a peck on the cheek.

I wanted to tell her it was wonderful, fantastic, sensational, *astounding* to have her back, but in my quietly thrilled state, all those big words might have got my tongue in a tangle. So "nice" would have to do for the moment, feeble as it was.

"Hello, Joanna!" said Becca, appearing shyly by my side.

(I'd never been able to bring myself to call Becca's parents Brian and Sue, probably because I sensed they'd really prefer me *not* to, even though they'd suggested it in the first place.)

"Hello, Becca! And lovely to see you too!"

We were all smiling fit to burst. Even the usually stern Krystyna had a faint hint of an upturned u-shape playing at her mouth.

"You know something, Heather?" Mum said excitedly, reaching out and holding one of my hands in both of hers.

"What?"

(My heart began to race – was this something to do with Dad? I still hadn't heard back from him about meeting up. Maybe that was because he was planning to get back together with Mum?)

"Now that it's over between me and your Dad –"

(Ah, well, that was a no, then.)

"– it's all going to change," Mum announced, with unsettling zeal in her eyes. I was suddenly reminded of a documentary about a shouty American minister in the deep South, who ranted and raved about God and whoever till the whole congregation starting whooping and hallelujahing and fainting in happiness in front of him.

"What's going to change?" I asked in a small voice.

"*All* of it! You'll see!"

Uh-oh. She'd been talking big life stuff, and not next week's cleaning materials with Krystyna, obviously. I wasn't so grateful to Krystyna, all of a sudden. I just hoped she wasn't an undercover recruitment officer for a scary religious cult. . .

I was trying to shake a reply out of my cluttered head, to say I didn't really *want* things to change, I wanted them to get back to normal, thank you, when Mum spoke again.

"But first things first," she said, letting go of me with one of her hands and rummaging in the pocket of her loose grey trousers. "I promise I will never, *ever* forget your birthday again, Heather!"

"Oh, that's OK!" I shrugged, meaning it. Who cared about dumb, April Fool birthdays at the best of times, never mind when there were more important, fall-out-from-Bombshell events going on.

"I feel just terrible for forgetting! But I didn't even know what the date was, or the *month* was, till I looked at the calendar earlier," said Mum apologetically, glancing down at a something in her hand. "Now, I haven't been able to get to the shops to buy you anything –"

(Yeah, well, *that* wasn't exactly news.)

"– but in the meantime I thought you might like this: a pearl for a Pearl!"

I felt her slip the old ring on my finger.

Great.

A ring that I can't say I exactly liked, connected with a name I completely loathed.

"Eek!"

Becca's squeal of horror made me jump. I mean, the ring wasn't *that* bad. . .

"Becca, this is Sylv," said my mum, ever the hostess, as my school uniform-wearing best mate got her breath back after her first, close-up, surprise sighting of our house guest, in all her pale-faced, black-lipsticked glory.

Now I just had to figure out if Becca had broken her promise of not speaking to Sylv.

I mean, was "Eek" what you might call a word. . .?

**From:**     **wombat**

**Subject:**  **Happy Anniversary**

**Date:**     **Monday 9 April**

**To:**       **rsmith@smiledentalgroup**


Hi Dad

Happy Anniversary* – it's two weeks today since you left. Did you know that? You still haven't mentioned where you're staying. And you still haven't got back to me about meeting up.
    Love
    Heather x

* Should that be "*Un*-happy Anniversary"?

## Suitably gloomy pants

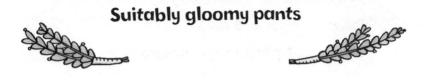

OK, so your standard real-life heroes are people like doctors and ambulance men and police officers and firefighters. Hurrah to them for saving people from accidents and illnesses and and bad guys and towering infernos.

But since I was a little kid, I've had a different kind of real-life hero – the blokes who work on refuse lorries. Yeah, those big, burly, no-messing blokes. It's not just 'cause they keep the streets clean, it's also 'cause they have squashy sentimental hearts underneath all that burliness.

Don't believe me?

Well, how come they feel the urge to rescue all these abandoned toys from the jaws of their crushers?

I was three when the hero worship first started. I'd spotted a huge grey lorry parked up outside the shops, where blokes with thick gloves and giant muscles were chucking the contents of black bins into the back of the metal-grinding crusher.

"Oi!" one of them shouted to the driver. "Fancy another mascot?"

"Yeah, go on, then," said the surly driver, breaking out in a slushy grin.

And up was thrown a three-legged panda, in shades of black and, well, *grey*.

It was then that I spotted what was tied on the front of the flat, ugly box of a lorry: a row of one-eyed, limbless, filthy, once-adored teddies and similarly wonky fluffy fuzzballs.

I was instantly charmed, and pretty soon after became a rescuer of unloved or lost soft toys too. I mean, just 'cause something's a little scuzzy around the edges, it doesn't deserve to be dumped, does it? In fact, it's probably more in need of hugs than your average toy. *And* it's got history – unlike some neatly pelted brand-new teddy from Toys" Я "Us.

Anyway, that's why I've ended up with a collection of fifty-one, and counting. It's the only one of my collection crazes I've stuck with. Mum says I've got rescue-toy radar; I can spot a desperately waving paw or a despondent furry ear from a mile off.

But there *is* an etiquette, even with scuzzy toys. I mean, you see a muddy pink bunny, and you have to think, *Some little kid might love that; some little kid might not be able to sleep at night without it*, so you must always stick it safely on a nearby wall and give it a day, in case anyone comes back to reclaim it. If it's still there, then (according to the law in my head) it's coming home with me, destined for a whirl around in the washing machine and a place among the piles of rescuees that line the shelves of my room.

Speaking of soft toys. . .

"La, la, la, la, LAH!!" trilled Tallie, making her teddy – Mr Boo – dance on the back of the seat in front of us.

"*Don't*, Tallie!" I said softly, realizing that the man sitting there wasn't too bear-friendly. His bald head kept moving irritably as he kept a check on how close my sister's bear was pirouetting towards his shoulder.

"But Mr Boo's just excited about going to this ballet shop . . . work thing, same as me!" said Tallie defensively, flopping back against the chequered material of the bus seat. Tallie loved her ballet, same as I loved throwing myself around in the privacy of my bedroom, to anything loud and fast. Maybe in our own ways, we both took after our great-granny Pearl, the one who died of dancing (yep, I'll get round to that some time, when my head is less cluttered).

"It's a ballet *workshop*. And I know you and Mr Boo are excited, but you have to think about other people," I reminded Tallie, pulling her bear away from the silver bar of the bus seat.

Me and Tallie were headed for the Yvonne Swanley Ballet School, where Mum (usually) took Tallie every Saturday morning. "While everything's changing," Mum had said to us yesterday, with that strange glint in her eye, "I need help from all of you." She wouldn't elaborate on the changes, and I was too nervous to push her on what they might be. All I *did* do was agree to take Tallie to this holiday workshop today, as Mum needed to be out and about in the car "doing" stuff. I didn't mind; watching a bunch of little girls galumph around pinkly was pretty cute, and riding on the top deck of the number eleven bus was much nicer than being stuck inside Mum's awful, size-of-an-elephant 4x4, which she could never manage to park anywhere except the driveway of our house.

"Mr Boo says you're *no* fun," Tallie growled, holding her bear to her ear.

"Yeah, well, tell Mr Boo that if there's any more moaning, I'm going to lock him in *here*!" I teased her, holding up her pink ballet kit case with its oversized clasp.

"But Mr Boo *always* likes to watch me dance!" gasped Tallie, clutching the bear tightly to her chest.

She knows when I'm only joking; she really does.

But I wasn't so sure Yvonne Swanley would be breaking into a warm, welcoming smile at the sight of Tallie's normally pristine bear today. Mr Boo's candy-pink neck ribbon was gone, lost somewhere in the muddle of Tallie's formerly immaculate bedroom (hey, welcome to the swamp of toys). And he was filthy, thanks to Tallie using him face-first to clean raindrops and mud off the slide in the playpark yesterday. Actually, that's what had got me thinking of my fifty-one lost toy souls – Mr Boo looked more like he should be a resident of my rescue shelves, instead of hanging out with a bunch of wannabee Sugar Plum Fairies.

And I wasn't so sure Yvonne Swanley would be breaking into a warm, welcoming smile at the sight of Tallie either. Normally my sister would pitter-patter into class, glossy blonde sweep of neatly brushed hair held back with a pale pink hairband. Today, her loose hair was adorned with three mouse-nest-sized tangles (it had been a week since she'd let anyone near her with a brush) and two twinkly black bat clips (borrowed from guess who).

"Hey, Tallie," I said, suddenly remembering I had something important to ask her.

"Not talking to you," she answered, hunkering her head into Mr Boo and pretending to be in a huff.

"Did *you* cut Dad out of the photo of us on the pinboard?" I continued, ignoring her huff.

The photo on the pinboard in the kitchen: it had been taken at a beachside restaurant in Greece last year; a snap-shot moment of a good-looking, lightly tanned family, with me hovering at the edge, lightly sunburnt. The waiter who'd taken the photo had kept telling Dad what a beautiful family he had, without ever making eye contact with me. He might be surprised to know that one member of Dad's beautiful family had hacked him crudely out of the sunny scene.

"No," Tallie muttered, without lifting her face from Mr Boo.

"Oh, OK." I shrugged, and gazed out of the window opposite.

I didn't have to solve the mystery right this second. I had plenty of other things to think about, like why Dad still hadn't been in touch about meeting up yet, and what kind of underwear goths wore.

I don't mean to sound like someone with a weird obsession with underwear – it was just that I spotted Sylv filling the washing machine this morning and got to thinking that goths couldn't just settle for a three-pack of M&S high-leg white knickers, could they? Was there some kind of specialist undies catalogue they could get stuff from? Maybe a catalogue where they order a three-pack of black hipsters, one patterned with pentangles, one with spiders and one with skulls. Nice. . .

"Mumfle-mumf-mumff," Tallie suddenly mumbled, disturbing my disturbing thoughts of suitably gloomy pants.

"What?" I leaned over, trying to make out the mumble.

"*Jo-Jo* did it," said Tallie, "But I lent him my safety scissors, 'cause he couldn't find any."

For someone who said he didn't want to think about Dad, Jo-Jo had been doing plenty of negative, Dad-related craftwork recently. There was the "WORLD'S WORST DAD" mug; a graffiti of rude words scrawled across a brochure for Dad's dental surgery, and now this.

"OK, but don't go lending him any more scissors," I said gently, not wanting Tallie to think I blamed her for it, and making a mental note to move the photo albums under the coffee table to a place of refuge, in case my brother got itchy fingers again any time soon.

*Bleep!*

A text; I rummaged in the top pocket of my jacket and pulled out my mobile.

"It's Becca!" I lied in a slightly delirious voice, when I saw Dad's message ping up.

Tallie didn't seem to notice. She was starting to unfurl, and was now rummaging around for something or other in her own jacket pocket.

"*Sorry, Heather – everything crazy, so haven't been in touch. How about meeting right now? Could be at the café by the park gates in ten minutes?*"

Ohhhh . . . the idea of sitting with Dad, listening to the voice that was as soothing as hot chocolate on a cold day; the voice that was meant to calm patients so that they fought their natural urge to leap away as soon as a shrill drill came anywhere near them.

Ohhhh . . . to be sitting in that café by the park, where Dad took us so often when we were growing up, as an alternative to the one *in* the park, which he said was too full of chattering women, whiny babies, and the occasional, corny, singalong-nursery-rhyme session, which was exactly the sort of thing that made Dad grind his perfect teeth.

Ohhhh . . . to see him face to face, to hear *his* side of the story, and maybe understand better what made him leave the family behind, where it was gently disintegrating.

Ohhhh . . . I couldn't make it – not with Tallie in tow. If it was a toss between ballet and Dad, ballet was bound to win for her. Actually, at the moment, if it was a toss between licking slugs and seeing Dad, I'd put money on the slugs. . .

"*Can't,*" I keyed back. "*I'm on other side of town, taking Tal—*"

"OI!!"

I jumped so hard that I accidentally pressed a button and sent the unfinished text as it was.

Dad would be frowning now, wondering what I was trying to say, and why I hadn't finished saying it.

But, hey, I was slightly distracted by the furious face of the bald man in front of us. His eyes were bulging, and he looked ready to reach across and throttle my little sister.

"I didn't mean to!" Tallie squeaked, her frightened

eyes suddely locked on mine, a red felt pen clutched in her hand.

"Didn't mean it, my @*$%!" swore the bald man, turning round long enough to show me the back of his head. "What's she drawn on it?"

"It's-only-a-squiggle-I'm-very-sorry-but-this-is-our-stop," I gabbled at high speed, as I grabbed up our belongings and unceremoniously shunted Tallie out of our seat and along towards the stairs.

"But—" blustered the angry bald man.

"It'll wash off!" I called out as we disappeared to the bottom level, frantically ringing the bell. "Our mum only buys her non-indelible pens!"

Non-indelible pens. . . I sounded like a desperate stationery salesperson, instead of what I was: a desperate sister.

"Tallie!" I snapped at her as soon as the bus doors closed and we found ourselves safely on the pavement with – thankfully – no enraged bald man following us and only – ha! – a two-kilometre hike to ballet class. "Have you gone *completely* mad?"

Tallie's tense face suddenly morphed into a wicked giggle.

Actually, *I* was the mad one for even asking that question. My whole family had gone mad – hadn't I noticed? My schoolboy brother had turned into an accommodation letting agent and my mum was a convert to some strange Polish (or Estonian?) religious cult and thought nothing of her five-year-old cutting up books and her son moving strangers with weird pants into our home. Speaking of home, the minute I was back I was going to make a sign for my bedroom door: *"SANE ZONE – only enter if sane!". That's* what I'd write.

Then I noticed the expression on Mr Boo's furry face.

He was currently being squashed in a hug by the neck, and seemed to be looking at me in beady-eyed desperation.

You know something? I probably looked much the same. . .

Hi Dad

Sorry I sent a sawn-off text earlier.

Had to take Tallie to a ballet workshop and it was all a bit of a hassle. Was going to get back to you once Tallie was dancing, but she'd snuck a Halloween costume in her kit bag instead of her ballet stuff, and some of the other little girls were crying 'cause they didn't want to dance with a witch.

Anyway, picked up your latest text five minutes ago, so YES, PLEASE, would love to meet you at the café on Friday afternoon instead. Not going to mention it to Mum, if that's all right. Or is it? Do you want me to? Or not?

Sorry if I sound muddled. It's just that I am. Muddled, I mean.

Love

Heather x

## The mutant growl-squeak

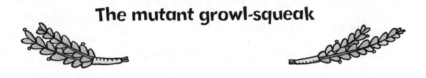

"You know, you're *always* getting colds, Heather," said Becca, stroking the once-velvety beak of a rescue duck on my bedroom shelves (found on the steps outside Woolworth's, 1998).

"I know," I replied with a voice that came out as a mutant growl-squeak.

My throat was so sore that it wasn't just my *throat* that hurt. The raw, shards-of-glass pain extended up from my throat, right the way into my nasal cavities, so that it even hurt when I *breathed*.

But it was nice. Not the searing pain, I mean, or those bizarre thoughts that kept drifting into my germ-addled mind about nasal cavities and sinuses. (Did you know that you've got sinuses in *loads* of places inside your head? Great big pouches of air, capable of hoarding a ton of snot each. It's amazing there's any room for your *brains* in there.)

What I mean was it had been nice just cuddling up in bed all day, having Mum bring me Lemsips and topped-up hot-water bottles, and asking if I was all right, honey.

If I blocked out the world beyond my bedroom walls, I could almost imagine that everything was just as it usually was. Now that it was late afternoon, Jo-Jo would be in his room, listening to unfeasibly loud music on his headphones, while breezing through unfeasibly difficult biology assignments, already on his way to being a dentist, same as Dad. Tallie would be quietly singing "Polly put the kettle on" as she poured tea for an immaculate, peach-faced Barbie and chums. Mum would be in the kitchen, fresh from a hard day's waft around her friend Lorraine's shop, and Dad would be finishing his last client of the day at the surgery, about to tidy up and come home to us.

Course, the real, post-Bombshell world wasn't like that at *all*.

"Hey, that Sylv girl is helping Tallie do something *very* weird to her teddy. . ." Becca said darkly, as she strolled over to my telescope and let her fingers drift through the necklaces dangling from it.

I don't know whether it was the weight of my jewellery or the sheer lack of use that had made my telescope wilt, slipping its gaze from the twinkly potential of stars in the skylight window to the piles of teen mags on my carpet.

"What sort of weird thing?' I growl-squeaked.

Becca seemed to have got over her shock at Sylv's sheer goth-ness last week. She said the bad dreams had only lasted a couple of days, anyway.

"Come and see for yourself," said Becca, lifting a piece of red ribbon from the telescope; an old bit of ribbon that I'd slipped the pearl ring on to so I wouldn't lose it. "Your mum said tea would be ready by now."

Idly looking at the ring, Becca walked over and slipped the ribbon over my tousled head.

"Don't think I'll go down. I'm not hungry," I mumbled weakly, as I stared down at the homemade necklace.

It seemed a waste to miss one of Mum's great meals (*I was still having recurring nightmares about never-ending beans on toast*). Still, I hadn't the energy to take the stupid pretend necklace off, never mind get out of bed and hobble woozily down the stairs.

"But your mum asked me to stay for tea!" said Becca, all hurt and disappointed all of a sudden. "*And* she said it was going to be a bit of a family conference!'

Horrible cold or no horrible cold, I could hardly miss out on a family conference, could I? Though it did seem kind of weird that Mum would invite Becca to stay if it was supposed to be a family conference, didn't it?

But then nothing was very surprising at the moment. Only *normal* would be surprising.

"Surprise!" said Mum, grinning broadly and holding her arms out wide so I could behold the spread on the table.

"Is it a party?" asked Becca, as we both slipped on to the last two chairs gathered round the dining table.

"No." Mum laughed. "But then maybe it *is*, sort of!"

It was an easy mistake to make on Becca's part. A new paper tablecloth printed with retro-Fifties roses on it covered the expensive, highly polished surface that was usually on show. There were fat white candles (could start a successful fire, if tipped on the paper tablecloth). There were lots of bowls of nibbly things to eat, instead of Mum's usual Jamie Oliver-inspired cooking. There was juice in our chunky glasses. Which *might* sound normal, apart from the fact that they had paper umbrellas stuck in them. . .

"What are *these* for, Joanna?" Becca asked Mum,

picking out a lemon-yellow one and twirling it in her fingers.

"Fun!" Tallie burst in, making a worryingly punk'd Mr Boo dance a kind of Highland Fling across an overlapped fork and knife.

"Exactly! For fun!" Mum beamed, nodding at Tallie. "Something I think we need more of round here!"

"Definitely." Jo-Jo nodded in agreement.

"Is that *eyeliner*?" Becca gasped, spotting Jo-Jo's new look for the first time.

"Maybelline," said Sylv, hastily pulling a kohl pencil out of the pocket of her black combats and holding it out towards a puzzled Becca, who was coming to terms with a shock discovery about her idol, rather than looking for make-up tips at the time.

"Well, isn't this nice!' Mum announced, as she smiled at us all.

And when I say "all", I better tell you the guest list in full at this "family" conference;

Mum: in jeans. Mum *never* wore jeans. Well, maybe in the far-off days when she and Dad went backpacking round Thailand and Mexico and wherever, but not within living memory for me. And that tight red T-shirt and trashy red fake flower stuck in her hair – she didn't buy *those* with her staff discount at Lorraine's posh clothes shop.

Me: resplendent in oversized polka-dot PJs and a red runny nose.

Jo-Jo: eyeliner, sudden cocky attitude, T-shirt with "I *could*, but I won't" printed across the chest.

Sylv: head-to-toe in black, except for the streak in

her hair that she'd now dyed red, with a red stud in her nose to match.

Tallie: an extra bird-nest tangle or two in her hair. Chunky bracelets and loads of rings on each hand – all drawn on in royal blue ink. (*Please* let it be wash-off. *Please* let the red pen yesterday be wash-off too. I'd been lying – my new favourite hobby – when I'd told the man on the bus it was.)

Krystyna: our cleaner/Mum's saviour/potential cult leader/now our Wednesday-night dinner guest.

Mr Boo: in a deliberately ripped pink T-shirt with a pierced furry ear, and eyeliner drawn on in marker pen.

Becca: her usual, pretty, perfect self, which made her the odd one out round the table this tea time.

"Dive in!" Mum ordered, pointing at the bowls of food. "I thought tapas would be fun for a change!"

"Fun": that was Mum's word of the day, though I didn't feel like I was in a "fun" mood myself – I was too spaced out with my cold and general confusion for that.

"What does tapas mean, Mum?" asked Tallie, happily digging into a pile of shiny green olives with one spoon and tomato-y potatoes with the other.

"It's a Spanish way of serving food in interesting small portions. Like the meze we had in Greece last year. Remember?"

For just a fleeting second, Mum's face crumpled a little, her red lips pursed. She was picturing Dad, I knew she was. That time Dad was eating the calamari, maybe, while I gave him a lecture on how calamari was octopus and it was terrible to eat octopuses because research showed they were so smart that their tentacles could think independently of their brain. (I thought that was a very useful and interesting thing to know, until Jo-Jo pointed out that calamari is actually *squid*.)

"We have little food like this in Poland," Krystyna suddenly interjected. "Some time I will make you some *fasolka po bretonsku*. You will love it."

All of us smiled politely and said nothing. We were too busy wondering what *fasolka po bretonsku* might be, and so unused to hearing Krystyna make conversation that we didn't think to ask.

"Um, super!" said Mum, regaining her composure and lifting up her chunky glass. "Anyway, I'd like to make a toast. Here's to the future!"

I lifted my glass about two centimetres off the table, while everyone else held theirs high and clunk-chinked them together.

It just felt a bit corny, and anyway, I didn't exactly know what Mum meant.

For about two seconds anyway.

And then I discovered the future was all about *salsa*, for goodness' sake.

"It's been three weeks, well, nearly a month now since your dad's been gone, and while I was . . . in my room, I did a lot of thinking," said Mum, gazing round at us. "I reappraised my life. I thought a lot about – about the girl I used to be, and how I'd somehow lost her along the way. The girl I used to be, well, she loved to travel, and dance and laugh. The girl I used to be wouldn't have been in the least bit bothered about having a big house and a big car and expensive clothes. It's like I've managed to forget what's important in life!"

Urgh, what Mum was saying half gave me a lump in my throat and half made me squirm 'cause it sounded like a script from a bad film. And apart from the corniness, what she was saying made me feel slightly nervous. Would the girl Mum "used to be" be in the least bothered about having three kids?

"So I'm hoping that you guys can be patient with me for a little while longer, while I figure some stuff out," Mum said, smiling hopefully at me, Jo-Jo and Tallie. "Anyway, here's to a a shiny, new future for all of us, with lots more fun!"

Mum raised her glass again. I raised mine higher this time, in case she thought I wasn't being supportive. Then I nervously took a sip of juice – and got a parasol in my left eye.

"*Oooooofffff!*"

"Are you OK, Heather?" I heard Mum ask, her voice getting closer as the pain seared my eye.

Great. My family was about to set off into a shiny, new future, full of fun, and I was going to be blind in one eye.

"Can you open it?" Mum's voice asked again.

It was the strangest thing; my right eye had come out in sympathy with my injured left one and both were streaming so much that the looming faces of my family seemed to be staring in at me a metre-deep in a choppy sea. A blurry Sylv spoke next.

"It's fine – it's not scratched. She just needs something cold on it to calm any swelling down."

Nurse Sylv. I thought goths were more into Dracula and depressing music than first aid.

"Good idea," said a blurry Mum, with the blur of red rose bobbing in her hair. "I'll go and get a wet flannel. . ."

"No – you've got to leave for your salsa class soon. *I'll* look after her."

And that's how I found myself being led to the kitchen, having an ice-cube wrapped in a tea towel pressed to my face, and beginning my first ever conversation with the girl from Jo-Jo's bedroom. . .

"What did you mean, about salsa?" I asked, feeling slightly delirious.

"You're mum's going to a salsa dance class tonight. Krystyna's a big fan, and thought it would do her good."

Yet another unexpected side to Krystyna's personality. I wouldn't be surprised to hear she was an expert lion tamer and planned to audition for the next series of *The X Factor*.

"Mum's going out?!" I growl-squeaked.

I mean, I knew Mum was going out and about during the day; you could tell there'd been trips to the supermarket from the healthier state of the fridge and kitchen cupboards. But going out dancing at *night*? Dad had only been gone five minutes. It wasn't that I expected her to stay in mourning for our old family life for ever and ever amen, but grooving around to sexy Latin music seemed a bit sudden, in a giddy, kind of over-excitable way.

Sylv might have shrugged a reply, but I couldn't see 'cause of the cold tea towel slapped across my eyes.

"But Jo-Jo's got his squash club!" I said, realizing that meant Tallie and I were going to be home alone.

"Squash club?!" I heard Sylv splutter.

"Yes, squash club!" I answered defensively. "Who's going to look after us?"

It was a dumb thing to say, in the circumstances – the circumstances being that I always hated Mum and Dad making out that Jo-Jo needed to babysit me and Tallie whenever they went out. (I didn't play with matches; I wasn't going to eat any paracetamols, thinking they were sweets; I wasn't going to let psychotic strangers into the house to murder me and my little sister.)

I knew I sounded childish, but I couldn't help it. I suddenly *felt* well and truly childish.

"*I* will," I heard Sylv say. "I offered to babysit, 'cause I'm not starting back at work till tomorrow night."

It was time to come out from under the tea towel. Holding the dripping lump of icy-cold material, I squinted at Sylv with my good eye.

"You work?" I growl-squeaked.

I was shocked enough at the idea that Mum had left this practically unknown person in charge of me and my sister, but I was actually more shocked at the idea of Sylv working somewhere. I mean, you never get goth teachers, or goth librarians, or goth bus drivers, do you?

"Yeah – I work behind the bar at the Coach and Horses. It's where I met your brother."

Sylv blithely batted her black-rimmed eyes at me.

"But – but the Coach and Horses is a *pub*!"

A pub in the centre of town that looked grubby from the outside, not like one of those posh gastropubs that Mum and Dad sometimes took us all to for Sunday lunch. From the outside, the Coach and Horses looked a lot like the sort of pub that would be filled with old men who talked about horse-racing and sat on beer-sticky bar stools till the barmen kicked them out (that's what Dad joked about it once, anyway). My trendy, clean, underage, seventeen-year-old brother didn't hang out in a place like *that*, did he?

"Yeah, well technically it *is* a pub, but it's more of a music venue." Sylv shrugged. "Monday and Wednesday nights are the indie band nights; those are the nights Jo-Jo comes, of course."

Of course.

In this parallel universe that I was now inhabiting, my brother didn't go to school squash club and karate; he secretly hung out watching indie bands in a pub. I kept thinking nothing could surprise me any more, but the surprises just kept coming.

"And the downstairs room is where they do the dance classes," Sylv continued. "It's salsa on a Wednesday. I know Krystyna from there."

"But Mum . . . Mum might bump into Jo-Jo there!" I said in a panicky whispered growl-squeak.

Sylv narrowed her eyes at me, as if she was trying to figure out what point I was trying to make.

"Well, she's giving him a lift, so I guess you *could* say she'll bump in to him!" she replied.

"Mum *knows* Jo-Jo hangs out in a pub?!"

In my old life – in my family's old life – my parents would have grounded Jo-Jo for about a *year* if he came home with so much as the faintest whiff of beer on him.

"Er, yeah, I guess," said Sylv, with a shrug.

And I guessed Mum and Jo-Jo must have been doing

quite a lot of chatting and sharing recently. And I guessed that "in the grand scheme of things", Mum must have decided that along with moving girls into his room, Jo-Jo hanging out in smelly, noisy pubs was OK.

"*That's* pretty," I heard Sylv say, through my fug of muddle-headedness.

She was holding up the pearl ring dangling from the ribbon round my neck.

"Uh . . . so's yours," I said, finding myself looking at the broken-heart necklace, and not sure what else to say till the muddle un-fuddled in my brain.

"What's the story behind this?" asked Sylv, holding the pearl in the middle of her palm.

"It, um, belonged to my great-granny Pearl. She died of dancing. But that's another story. What about yours?"

Sylv rubbed the broken heart between the fingers of her other hand.

"I got it from a bad boyfriend. It didn't used to be broken. But that's another story."

Sylv smiled gently, like she was teasing, but in a nice way.

"Maybe we should swap stories later, once everyone's gone?" she suggested.

Maybe we should.

And maybe if we were going get all buddy-ish and swap stories, we should ease our way in to our new buddy-ish state by clearing up a small mystery first.

"Can I ask you something, Sylv?" I growl-squeaked.

"Sure?"

"Why do you keep your nail varnish in the fridge. . .?"

Hi Dad

Nail varnish lasts longer if you keep it in the fridge, and it stops it from going all gloopy. Just thought you might like to know – ha!

Can I just tell you again that I can't wait till Friday?

Got to go. Sylv is babysitting me and Tallie tonight and I think she might be interesting to talk to.

Might email again before I go to bed.

Love

Heather

## Death by dancing

Goth-ed.

We'd been well and truly goth-ed.

Well, I guess you couldn't say Sylv had been goth-ed 'cause she already *was* one.

But me and Tallie, we'd spent the last hour in make-up heaven (or make-up hell, depending on how adventurous you were), and we both now had beautifully pallid skin (hid my red, cold-y nose), purple-y, eye-lined eyes and ruby-red lips outlined in smoky black. I didn't go for the bat on the cheek, like Tallie. Oh, no. I was *much* more sophisticated and chose a cobweb on my left cheek. (*Wow*, it tickled when Sylv was painting it on.)

The sheer excitement of being goth-ed finally took its toll on Tallie (or maybe it was the fact that she was up two hours after her bedtime) and she fell asleep – along with Mr Boo – across our laps. Me and Sylv's, I mean.

"Want to watch some TV?" I asked Sylv, now that we were pinned to the sofa.

"Sure," said Sylv, with a shrug of her black-netted shoulders.

The remote was just within grabbing distance, without lurching and disturbing Tallie too much.

"Er . . . maybe not!" I mumbled, flicking on to a channel and finding an old re-run of *Supernanny*. Me and Sylv looked at each other, glanced down at the sleeping goth-child and sniggered. What would Supernanny make of Tallie's childcare tonight? It was hardly nice-bath-followed-by-lovely-story-followed-by-all-tucked-up-cosy-in-bed.

Oops.

"She looks like an extra from some band's music video!" Sylv smiled at me, stroking a tangle of blonde hair out of Tallie's face.

"I guess so," I said, thinking I'd never seen any band's video that featured a kid as beautiful and frankly weird as Tallie looked tonight.

I let the remote bounce the TV over to a music channel, and pressed mute while a shouty rap band with big-boobed backing dancers did their shouty thing.

"Y'know, I've got loads of CDs and DVDs of bands I love. But they're all back at my mum's . . ." Sylv suddenly said ruefully, her eyes on the silent screen.

OK. Now that we were talking, now that I knew why she kept her nail varnish in the fridge, now that I knew her well enough to goth me up, I felt I could ask her a pretty obvious question.

"Um . . . why did you move in here?" I quizzed, putting it about as clunkily and unsubtly as Becca would've.

Sylv shrugged. She began to fiddle with her necklace, same as I fiddled and scratched at my nose when I was nervous. I was touching on a touchy subject, I realized.

"Well . . . my mum moved her new boyfriend and his two bull terriers into our flat. Thing is, I'm allergic to dogs. And mum's boyfriend, Harry, is allergic to goths. So one of us had to go."

Right then and there, I developed a shock-o-meter. Behold my readings.

"*You* had to go?!" I said incredulously, 'cause of *course* it was Sylv who'd had to go, otherwise we'd have a bloke called Harry and his two big-jawed dogs living with us. OK, so we *wouldn't*, but you get what I mean.

[*Shock-o-meter reading: 8/10. I'd thought mums hibernating was hard enough to deal with, but mums who took sides with boyfriends called Harry with their scary-fanged dogs was terrible.*]

"Uh-huh." Sylv nodded. "I knew it wouldn't be great, us all living together, but I was hoping it would be all right for a while. Just for a few weeks, till I go to Camp America. But it just didn't work out that way."

"You're going to help out at kids' summer camps?!"

[*Shock-o-meter reading: 6/10. I'd heard of Camp America. Jade Stevens' big brother did it — taught kids to swim and abseil and other outdoorsy stuff. But were the children of America ready for a goth singing them songs round the campfire?*]

"Yeah, and then I'm going to Southampton University in October to do Marine Biology."

"That's where you learn about stuff like how to tell the difference between squid and octopus, right?"

[*Shock-o-meter reading: 6/10. Were the shrimps and plankton of the world ready for a goth fish scientist?*]

"*Kind* of," smiled Sylv. "I was meant to do all this a year ago, but my parents split up and it was all a bit . . . urgh. So I put it off and got the job in the pub instead."

[*Shock-o-meter reading: 8/10. Sylv had been through a Bombshell thing too?*]

"You said you met my brother at the pub. How long ago was that?" I asked. I wanted to know more about Sylv's own personal Bombshell, but felt too shy to ask that question, knowing how weird and raw the whole family fall-out felt for *me* at the moment.

"Don't know. . ." said Sylv, her neatly drawn black eyebrows furrowing at she considered my question. "Six or seven months, I suppose?"

[*Shock-o-meter reading: 9/10. My "perfect" brother Jo-Jo had been secretly skiving his sports classes for six months?*]

"Jo-Jo's such a cutie," Sylv continued, her face breaking into an impromptu smile.

A-ha. So *did* she have a thing for him? I scanned her face for obvious signs of Becca-style longing, but saw nothing. Seemed like she'd meant "cutie" in the same way as a big sis is fond of a kid brother.

"I mean, he's always been a great mate to me, and that hasn't been easy, since my ex —" at this point Sylv held up the necklace she'd been distractedly fiddling with "— is the lead singer in the band that Jo-Jo manages."

"Excuse me?" I growl-squeaked. Thank God I wasn't eating anything, because I might have choked.

[*Shock-o-meter reading: 9/10. Jo-Jo — my sports-mad, studying-so-he-could-be-a-dentist brother — was the manager of a band? Could seventeen-year-olds BE managers of bands?!*]

"Didn't you know?" Sylv frowned at me.

"Uh, no," I replied, feeling annoyed that Jo-Jo hadn't trusted me with his secret any time over the last half a year or so.

"Jo-Jo really stood up for me," Sylv drifted on, not really registering the stunned look on my face (maybe the goth makeover was hiding my true expression). "Specially when Ade chucked me the way he did."

Ade: the name of the bad boyfriend. The singer in the band Jo-Jo managed. (It was going to take a while for that last one to sink in.)

"How did your boyfriend chuck you, then?" I asked nosily.

"In a song," said Sylv matter-of-factly. "He just stood up on stage one night and sang the words right at me. It was called 'So Sorry, Sylvia'."

[*Shock-o-meter reading: 10/10. How mean would you have to be to let a person – and a whole pub-full of strangers – know they were chucked that way? At least Dad had the decency to tell Mum face-to-face in the shower-room.*]

"Anyway, that night, I unclipped my heart –" Sylv held up her silver pendant "– and I've worn it this way ever since. So now you know the story of my necklace. Want to tell me yours?"

After reeling from all the shocks, I was a bit stumped for a second, as I tried to search my brain for the snippets of info I knew about my great-granny Pearl.

"It's not too exciting," I began, as Sylv gently lifted the ring around my neck and studied it. "Pearl was my mum's granny. I think she was pretty eccentric. She was mad on entering competitions, and when she died, they found tons of stuff crammed in her house, like five unused kettles in their packaging and a drawer full of letters from travel companies saying stuff like '*Congratulations! You have won a coach trip for two to Latvia!*'"

"Well done her!" Sylv smiled.

"Yeah, but the funny thing was that she never went on any of the holidays; she'd never been abroad!" I said with a grin, remembering the family jokes about Pearl and her secret world of imaginary holidays.

And then my grin faded a bit when I thought what people would make of *my* room, if I died out of the blue. My piles of rubbish soft toys; the non-existent key-ring collection in a stupidly big box under the bed marked "*Keyrings – hands off!*"; the astronomy books covered in dust that I'd asked for for my birthday one year and then never opened; the seven scrapbooks full of dumb *Far Side* cartoons. *Who* exactly was the crazy person in our family tree?

"You know how loads of women worked in factories during the Second World War, when the men were away fighting?" I carried on, my brain trawling up another fact about Pearl. "And you know how clothes were rationed back then, and you couldn't hardly buy anything new and pretty?"

"Uh-huh." Sylv nodded.

"Well, Pearl worked in a parachute factory, and she *loved* to dance. Apparently, she took all the remnants of silk that the parachutes were made from and sewed a dress for herself to go dancing in."

"Brilliant!" laughed Sylv, jiggling Tallie slightly, though she didn't wake. "I can picture Pearl now, swirling around a dancefloor to some Glenn Miller tune. . ."

I nodded, though I had no idea who Glenn Miller was. I'd look him up later in the *British Book of Hit Singles and Albums*, if he wasn't too long ago to be in there.

"Actually, it *wasn't* so brilliant," I said, remembering the most unique thing about Pearl. "She actually *died* of dancing."

"Died of dancing?!" Sylv frowned at me again. "How does *that* work?"

"She lived in sheltered housing when she was really old. They were always having dance nights," I began to explain. "She was meant to take it easy 'cause she was so old and everything, and her heart wasn't that great. But she always danced to every song, dragging up all the old guys there one by one."

I paused for a second, remembering what Mum had mentioned about the ring being given to Pearl by someone who wasn't my great-granddad – I must ask Mum to tell me more about that one of these days.

"Anyway, one night, she'd dragged up every single guy, and even some of the women to waltz with her, or whatever that kind of dancing is called," I carried on, "and it got to the last track of the night. The old guy she had as a partner thought she was leaning backwards, 'cause she wanted him to dip her. You know what I mean?"

Sylv nodded. She knew I meant that sort of swooping down-and-back-up move that ballroom dancers show off with.

"So anyway, this old guy dipped her. But she hadn't wanted to be dipped at all. She'd just died in his arms of dancing."

"*That*," said Sylv, opening her eyes wide till their pale blueness pointed at me like laser beams, "is the best way I have *ever* heard to die. Excellent!"

At that second, I had a profound thought. Which was pretty unusual for me, since my thoughts tended to be more along the lines of gibberish.

And that profound thought was that I'd resented Sylv without really knowing her, just 'cause I needed to be grumpy with someone. And that the someone I needed to be grumpy with was Dad, only he wasn't around to be grumpy with, if you see what I'm saying. (See? I can even turn a profound thought into gibberish.)

And now that I'd got Dad on the brain . . . it occurred to me that it was only two days till I was going to meet him in the café by the park. How was that going to feel? Was I going to want to hug him? Or grab the sugar bowl and pour it over his head?

I hoped my heart wouldn't be pounding as fast as it was right now, just *thinking* about my Dad-date.

I didn't want to go dying of a high-speed heart attack before I got the chance to give him a cuddle – or a sugar shower . . .

**From:** **wombat**

**Subject:** **Jogging cows**

**Date:** **Wednesday 11 April**

**To:** **rsmith@smiledentalgroup**


Hi again, Dad

Did you know that. . .


- A herb called echinacea is very good for colds? (Sylv has some and I started taking it tonight, so I can be well enough to come meet you on Friday.)
- *Fasolka po bretonsku* is a Polish dish that's made out of butter beans, onion and tomato? (Me and Sylv looked it up on the internet.)
- Glenn Miller was as famous as Coldplay back in the 1940s? His most famous song was called "In The Mood". I downloaded it from iTunes and me and Sylv danced around the room to it, even though we weren't very sure how you were meant to dance to that kind of music.


Oh, that reminds me; I'm going to download a track Sylv was talking about, called "Swimming Horses", by a band called Siouxsie and the Banshees. She says it's very atmospheric. I kind of got the giggles though, wondering if the rest of their music was called stuff like "Jogging Cows" and "Skating Ducks". I'm glad I didn't say that out loud though, 'cause I know it's not very funny – it's just that I've

got snot clogging up the humour part of my brain.
    See you Friday!
    Love
    Heather x

# Step away from the sugar bowl. . .

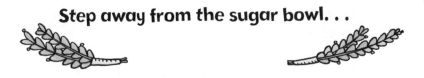

One small-but-important minute, that was all.

(*Thump-a-thump-a-thump-a-thump*, went my high-speed heart.)

It was Friday, it was 3.59 p.m., and I was only one small-but-important minute away from the café by the park, and – after nearly three weeks apart – only one small-but-important minute away from seeing Dad.

No one knew about me meeting him except Becca, who was keeping me company in case I got the wobbles (from nerves, or maybe blocked sinuses) while I was making my way there. Of course, when I say no one but Becca knew, that probably meant Mr and Mrs Fitzgerald knew too. "They *don't*!" Becca insisted. "They'd better not!" I warned her, thinking I might ban her from my house (and close-up sightings of Jo-Jo) if she accidentally went blabbing my secrets to her parents again.

"So, what do you think he'll say?" asked Becca.

I had no idea what Dad would say. The *thump-a-thump-a-thumping* in my chest was reaching epic proportions at the very thought of seeing him and hearing whatever it was he was going to say. And ninety-five per cent of me wanted to see him so badly that he could have recited the menu at me in the style of a news reader and that would be good enough. (The remaining five per cent was so furious with him that I'd have to step away from the sugar bowl as soon as I went in there.)

"Do you think he'll look any different?"

Like I mentioned before, Becca can say some very dumb things.

I mean, why would Dad look any different? Just 'cause he'd left home, it didn't mean he'd have had a *face* transplant or something.

Then again . . . didn't people turn white-haired overnight, when they'd had a terrible shock? Maybe the shock (and guilt) of deserting us would have turned Dad's grey-tinged brown hair to platinum overnight. Or then there was that really pretty presenter off the telly; the girl who got alopecia when she was going through the stress of a divorce. . . But I didn't want to think about the "d" word, not just yet.

Maybe Dad wouldn't have been eating properly. Maybe, like Mum, he'd have lost so much weight from a gloom-induced diet that he'd be a shadow of his former self.

Maybe I'd walk into the café, and go right past him, not realizing that the sunken, wizened, bald man in the window seat was actually my dad. . .

(*Thump-a-thump-a-thump-a-thump*, went my high-speed heart.)

"It's funny how Sylv's in the same boat as you, isn't it? Not having a dad, I mean!" said Becca, skipping right on to her next question, even if it was another clunky one.

It's not as if me and Sylv didn't *have* dads. Sylv's, it turned out, was living in Spain, running a restaurant with his new wife, and mine was sitting in a café just round the corner.

"Oh! I can see him! I'm going to go now!" twittered Becca, squeezing my hand as we came within snooping distance of the café.

Sure enough – there he was.

(*Thump-a-thump-a-thump-a-thump*, went my high-speed heart.)

I was still a few metres away, but as Dad sat there staring into the coffee he was stirring, I was relieved to see that he wasn't sunken, wizened and bald at all. He was the same old Dad.

Er, kind of.

"Go for it!" Becca urged me, as she walked backwards and I stayed rooted to the spot. "Remember – things can only get better!"

Music. Music was always a good way of getting through things. I'd hummed my way through the entire score of *The Jungle Book* (at high speed) when I got my brace fitted, aged nine, which might have alarmed the dentist (Dad's partner) but definitely soothed *me*. Now I hummed Becca's birthday song as I forced my legs forward.

Dad must have had his daughter radar switched on: he lifted his head, grinned and waved at me.

Oh, wow, oh, wow, oh, wow.

"Hey, haven't we met some place before?" I goofed around, stepping into the café and trying to hide my nerves. (One look at the finger I was pointing his way and he'd've seen it was shaking so much it was in danger of dropping right off my hand.)

"Heather, honey," he murmured, standing up and wrapping me in a big, familiar hug.

I was happy, of *course* I was. Sort of *manic* with happiness, really. But I couldn't help doing the most nuts thing: even close up in this longed-for hug, I couldn't help checking him out. Checking out the fact that my hands were resting on the shoulders of a soft wool, round-neck jumper with thick bands of stripes on it. Not a baggy old guy's stripy jumper, but a kind of trendy, tight-fitting one. I'd never seen Dad in a trendy, tight-fitting stripy jumper *ever*. And I'd never seen him have his hair so casual, sort of combed floppily around his face. He smelled different too. Some citrus-y aftershave that I wasn't sure I liked. It reminded me of cat wee.

"It's *so* good to see you!" he said, ushering me down into the seat opposite him.

"Bet you remember me looking marginally better than this!" I goofed around again, pointing to my pale face and red, overblown nose.

"You look fine!" He grinned at me with his perfect teeth. "How are you, honey?"

His brown eyes bored into mine, as if they were trying to read every scrap of family-related info I had hidden in my head.

"Fine, apart from too much snot!" I goofed some more. "How are you?"

[Translation: "Are you thinking you might've made a mistake?", "Are you glad that you left us?", "Do you miss us more than you thought?", "Do you miss us *less* than you thought?"]

"Good, good. Hey – look at this . . . lucky sign or what?"

Dad pointed at the small vase on the table, filled with purple dried heather, of all things. He did a sort of cartoon scan of the room to make sure he wasn't being watched, winked at me, then pulled a couple of stems of heather out of the vase and handed them to me.

"Stick them in a jar or something when you get home, and every time you look at them, you can think of me!" he said with a grin.

"Thank you," I replied, feeling strangely shy as our fingers brushed together. "So . . . are you staying somewhere near here?"

"Ah, later, later," said Dad, shrugging off my question. "First, give me all the news from home. How's everyone? How's Tallie? I was a bit worried when you said she'd dressed up as a witch at her ballet workshop."

Truth, lies, truth, lies. Did I tell him quite how weird Tallie had been lately, or blur the facts a little?

"She's OK," I said with a shrug, buying myself some time.

"Still playing at tea parties?"

Well, she was, but she'd now ditched her dolls – blue-faced or otherwise – and was conducting her tea parties with guests of honour from my rescue shelves. This morning before breakfast, I'd seen my tail-less zebra (found 1999, outside the library), my eyeless leprechaun (found 1997, in bushes in the park), and the three-legged Eeyore (found 2000, in the gutter after a rainstorm) all sitting with punk'd Mr Boo, waiting for make-believe tea to be poured.

"Kind of."

All right, so I'd settled on a middle ground of not lying, but not telling either.

"And what about Jo-Jo?"

"He's fine. He's pretty . . . busy."

"Good, good. His exams aren't that far off," Dad said thoughtfully, as if he was glad to hear that his leaving hadn't thrown Jo-Jo off-course.

Of course, Jo-Jo wasn't busy with studying. I don't think he'd opened a page of his books the whole holiday so far. In fact, I hadn't seen much of him the past few days. According to Sylv, he was putting his band through rehearsals for a string of gigs he'd set them up with, starting with an opening act slot at a festival in the park in six weeks' time.

I found myself glancing out of the window, across the road to where the gig was going to take place. I really, *really* hoped Dad couldn't read my mind.

"And your mum? How is she?"

"She's . . . pretty good."

She was pretty late home from her salsa class the other night; I heard her trying to tip-toe in at 1.30 a.m., and then giggling to herself when she tripped over something left in our formerly spotless, now slightly grungy house.

"Has she done anything about that Sylv girl?" Dad asked, his face darkening slightly. "I really can't see how she thinks it's all right for Jo-Jo to go moving strange young women into our house. I know things must be hard, but she's still got to think about her parental responsibility, hasn't she?"

I got kind of *irked* then, and eyed the sugar bowl.

I'd never really been sure what irked meant till that second (it sounded like an antique word out of the 1950s, like "spiffing" and "crikey"), but it suddenly summed up the niggle of annoyance I felt. I mean, Dad hadn't shown much parental responsibility lately, had he? Moving out on us like he had? And since he *had* chosen to move out, he could hardly call it "*our*" house.

And another thing: a conversation – that's where two people take turns asking and answering questions, isn't it? Well, it seemed a bit one-sided at the moment. It seemed like only *Dad* was doing the asking and only *I* was doing the answering.

Time to ignore my thumping heart and get brave, I decided.

"Are you still off work?" I interrupted his monologue about Mum.

"Um, yes," he replied, looking faintly surprised to be stopped in his tracks. "I start back next week. I just needed a bit of time to get settled."

*Settled where?* I wondered.

"Settled where?" I boldly asked him.

"It doesn't matter." He shrugged, as if I'd just asked him a dumb question like what his favourite colour was, or asked him to count his knees or something.

Ooh, I was having another irked moment. Another eyeing-up the sugar bowl moment. Wow, this loving someone and being angry with them at the same time was *tough*.

"Jo-Jo doesn't believe you," I said, hoping I sounded cool and grown-up, when inside I felt *blah*.

"Jo-Jo doesn't believe *what* exactly?" asked Dad, sounding confused.

"That there's no one else involved. With you leaving, I mean."

Dad went pink-cheeked and white-faced and back again. Either he was guilty or annoyed – I just couldn't figure out which, till he decided to speak.

"That is just absolute rub—"

Sounded like the beginning of a denial, but he didn't get to the end of it because at that moment his phone burst into life, and Dad seemed to decide that answering his phone call was more important than sitting with one of his three children, after three weeks apart.

"Hello? Yeah, uh-huh. Uh-huh? Are you *sure*?"

Dad went pinked-cheeked and white-faced and back all over again.

"Uh . . . OK. I'll be right there."

Dad had promised to be right there. Wherever "right there" was. Which presumably wouldn't be *here*, with me, right now.

"Heather, honey," Dad said, clicking the call-end key on his mobile. "I'm sorry, but something's come up. I've got to cut this short."

I think I was meant to say something like "That's OK, I don't mind", but I didn't feel like it.

Being with Dad again. . . I'd been waiting for this particular moment for so long, but hadn't expected this particular moment to last for only a few minutes.

Dad hastily put some coins by his cup of coffee, and

then swooped over and gave me a slightly uncomfortable hug before I knew it.

"Oh, nearly forgot," he said, breaking away from me. "I've got you something. It's for one of your collections."

Dad was rummaging around in his jacket pocket. Stupidly, I went up on a little rollercoaster of emotion and felt all gushy about the fact that Dad always did seem that tiny bit more tolerant of my dumb stuff than anyone else. Hadn't he once brought home a mud-drenched dinosaur that he'd found outside the surgery?

"For those foreign coins you've got," he said, holding a small, beaded purse out to me.

Hmm. OK, two thoughts sprang to mind.

Call it bad timing, but I had started the coin collection years ago, just *after* most of our nearest neighbouring countries turned to the euro, which meant my coin collection consisted of an aforementioned euro, an American cent, an old Spanish peseta, and a British ten pence. Not a vast collection, then. Not one that warranted a specific purse.

And now for the second thought: the purse. . . It was the sort of plastic-beaded, butterfly-decorated diddy purse that I'd have loved – if I was *five*.

Thanks, Dad.

"Love you, sweetheart," he said, hurrying himself into his jacket and out of the café.

"Love you. . ." I muttered, not sure if he heard me, or if I really did. Love him, I mean.

As the door banged shut and the waitress walked towards our table to clear up, I fiddled with the sprigs of heather I had hidden in the palm of my hands.

And get this: I realized that hadn't even had so much as had a chance to *glance* at the menu, never mind order an orange juice or whatever.

Great to see you, Dad. . .

**From:** wombat

**Subject:** Squashed heather

**Date:** Friday 13 April

**To:** rsmith@smiledentalgroup

Hi Dad

Thanks for the birthday cheque I found inside the purse – not sure what I'll spent it on yet. I guess I'm not really in a shopping sort of mood right now.

By the way, I've stuck the heather from the café in the middle of the *British Book of Hit Singles and Albums*, as it's the thickest book I've got. When it's dried, I'll put it in a frame with that photo of you and me on the vampire ride at Chessington World of Adventures.

I'm feeling very tired.

Night, night.

Love

Heather x

## Guess what the Tooth Fairy brought

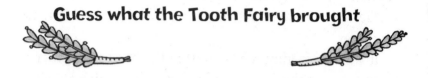

"I'm home!" I called out to whichever strange assortment of people might be in our house.

As it was a Monday, Krystyna might have been here in her professional capacity as our cleaner, but then again, she popped in pretty often these days, mostly to share stories of useless husbands with Mum (apparently hers ran off with the government official helping them apply for British citizenship, which sounds quite funny in an ironic way, but probably didn't feel very funny-ironic to Krystyna and her nearly grown-up kids at the time). And after only two sessions at salsa, Mum had already invited a couple of fellow salsa-ers (a Franny and a Zoe, both divorced with kids, spot the common thread!) for coffee and commiserating sessions.

Then, of course, there was Sylv and her huge suitcase, who was pretty good fun to have around, specially since Jo-Jo was off at band rehearsals all day and every day of the holiday.

"Anybody here?" I called from the hall.

Maybe they were out in the garden. It was pretty nice weather, and I could hear the distant shrieks of kids and barks of dogs as neighbours took advantage of the warm spring sunshine this tea time.

I was just putting my door keys into the tiny beaded purse – the only use I'd found for the gift Dad had given me when we met up a week or so ago – when I saw something I really didn't expect.

"Ta-daaa!" said Mum, bursting through the kitchen doorway.

It was all choppy, really short at the back with longer pointy bits at the front. It was a total rock-chick hairdo.

It's just that I'd never really thought of Mum as a rock chick before.

"Do you like it?" she asked, twirling round to give me a 360° viewing.

"Uh, yeah. . ." I said dubiously, thinking that I liked both Mum and the haircut, only perhaps not together. "Are those new too?"

On our first day back to school after the holidays, I thought Mum might be a bit lonely, rattling around the house on her own (well, I guess she had Sylv for company). I mean, although she was pretty up most of the time, she still had her down days, so I'd felt a little guilty for taking up Becca's offer of homework and snacks straight after school (chocolate digestives don't taste so good when you're guiltily thinking about your lonesome mum).

But instead of moping around forlornly, Mum had obviously busied herself with a trip to the hairdresser and a visit to the shoe shop. I'd quite fancied a pair of those biker-style boots myself, same as the ones Sylv sometimes wore, but my thirty-six-year-old mum had got in there first.

"Nice, aren't they?" she said, sticking a foot out and hauling her jeans up a little so I could see the buckle on them better. "Sylv helped me choose them. She helped me pick the hairstyle too. I didn't think I'd be brave enough to go for it, but I love it!"

"What about all the posh ladies in Lorraine's shop?" I asked, plopping the FatFace carrier bag – my lookalike schoolbag – down in the hallway. "Won't they be a bit . . . *freaked* by it?"

Mum hadn't been back to work in the month since The Bombshell, but she was getting better and better (with the occasional lapse of *not*-better thrown in), so I expected that it wouldn't be too long till she was wafting between the clothes rails, tweaking at ruffled hems and telling rich ladies that the emerald mohair was to die for.

Actually, you know when I said Mum was getting better and better (ish)? I didn't mean for anyone to think that meant she was getting more and more *normal*. Oh, no – part of her recovery seemed to involve her doing an unsettling amount of makeovers. She'd just about finished the wardrobe makeover (she'd loaded bin-bag after bin-bag of old clothes into our bus-of-a-car one day last week, all destined for the local charity shop). The house makeover was still in progress (the cream living-room walls were now painted a deep rose-ginger, Mum had bought an antique Turkish carpet called a kilim off eBay, and there was a huge, framed poster of this grand palace in Spain called the Alhambra on the wall, in the place where there used to be a small, abstract print that Dad liked).

And now the Mum makeover was complete.

Or maybe it was work in progress too. Maybe Sylv had her booked in for an auricle piercing and a Celtic knot tattoo on her bum tomorrow morning.

"Ah . . . the ladies at Lorraine's!" Mum laughed, doing this deep, throaty chuckle I'd never really heard her do before. "Well, I won't be subjecting them to my 'freaky' hair, 'cause I quit!"

"You quit your *job*?" I said, frowning at her. "But you love your job! And you've been friends with Lorraine for ages!"

"Yes, but have you seen her round here much?" Mum pointed out. "I've only spoken to her a couple of times, and she wasn't much help. You know your true friends if they support you through the tough times."

Were people like that? I guess so; Sylv had told me that her old mates were kind of useless when her parents split up. It was as if they were embarrassed or something, or like she had the plague – like they'd catch parents-splitting-up-itis. Maybe Lorraine was similarly spooked; maybe she thought her own husband would be infected with leaving fever if she came into direct contact with Mum. . .

Thank goodness for Becca. She might say the odd dumb thing, like "That purse your Dad gave you was really naff, wasn't it?", but at least she was always there for me.

"So, what are you going to do now?" I asked Mum. I didn't suppose we'd starve, or have to live on beans on toast (urgh) if Mum wasn't working. Once things were more settled, Dad would help out with money, for sure.

"It's fine!" said Mum gleefully. "I've got another job!!"

"Doing what?" I asked, slightly distracted by the clattering sound of Jo-Jo's old scooter getting dragged in through the French doors and over the slate tiles of the conservatory.

"Remember I dropped a whole load of my old clothes off at the charity shop last week?"

"Yeah, at Oxfam," I said, suddenly sussing that there was some kind of employment agency place next to Oxfam on the high street.

"Oh, no – I couldn't get parked anywhere near Oxfam, so I went down to the Animal Aid shop by the bus station car park."

The Animal Aid shop. . . I knew the one. It wasn't the sort of charity shop like Oxfam and those sort of places, where you can buy nicely-hung, hardly-worn jumpers and arty-crafty new ornaments and stuff. Animal Aid was the sort of old-fashioned charity shop that looked like it sold mostly clutter, dust and germs.

"*Well*," Mum said, eyes wide with the exciting secret she was about to spill, "I'm going to be the new manager! I saw they had an ad in the window, had an interview with them today, and I start next week!"

"You're going to work at the Animal Aid shop?" I checked in case I'd picked her up all wrong. I mean, Mum didn't do scuzzy. And Mum didn't do animals, apart from in nature documentaries on the TV.

But then again, I didn't realize she was a rock chick till thirty seconds ago.

"Yep!" Mum nodded enthusiastically, as if she'd just told me she'd been asked to be a stylist to the stars. "I really want to do something worthwhile!"

Sponsoring an African child was worthwhile. Campaigning against landmines in former war zones was worthwhile. I didn't know if working in an unsanitary dust emporium was exactly going to be worthwhile.

"Hezzer!" came a shout from the conservatory. "Come see *thish*!"

"Why's Tallie talking in that funny way?" I asked, stepping out of the hallway and into the living room.

"Oh, yes . . . she had a little accident today," said Mum, following me through.

I didn't worry when Mum said that; kids are *always* having little accidents. Well, maybe Tallie wasn't the sort of kid to have as many falling off walls/tumbling into ponds/skating into bollard incidents as *I* used to at her age, but it certainly wasn't anything to get worried about.

Or *was* it?

Tallie stood at the entrance into the conservatory, gripping the scooter and smiling broadly, showing off her perfect smile –

– minus one front tooth. . .

"She went hurtling head-first over her scooter when she was coming out of the school gates," said Mum, very matter-of-factly. "I whipped her down to hospital to check she didn't have concussion, but she was fine – apart from her front tooth coming clean out!"

"Does it hurt?" I asked, walking closer to inspect it.

"A bit. Not much. I think it was starting to get wobbly anyway. But look!" said Tallie.

"Yeah, I *am* coming to look," I told little Miss Impatient there. "Have you still got the tooth, Tallie? 'Cause you'll need it for the tooth fairy! I wonder what she'll bring you?"

Don't you just love the fact that you can cheer little kids up with all that Santa Claus and tooth fairy stuff when they're feeling –

"Hezza!" Tallie interrupted my musings. "*Look!!*"

Oh.

Tallie didn't want me to gawp at the gap in her mouth. Tallie was pointing down at something by her side.

A black and white, heavily panting something.

"Hish name'sh Tiago!" Tallie lisped prettily.

Good grief. I thought the tooth fairy brought money, or maybe sweets or small toys or something.

I had no idea she brought *dogs*. . .

**From:** wombat

**Subject:** Teeth and dogs

**Date:** Monday 23 April

**To:** rsmith@smiledentalgroup

Hi Dad

Here is today's news:

- Tallie lost a tooth – she crashed Jo-Jo's old scooter and it came right out, just like that.
- We now appear to have a dog. After all the years of me begging to have a puppy, and Mum saying no, dogs were too hairy and smelly, all it takes is for Tallie to lose a tooth, and suddenly Mum is shooting down to the dogs' home and picking up a dog that *was* called Timmy, but is now called Tiago, after Mum's Portuguese salsa teacher. (Did I tell you Mum's been going to salsa class?) I think he's a pretty cute dog, but I can't help feeling a bit *grrrrr* about it, if you see what I mean.
- Mum has a new job. She is going to be the manageress of the Animal Aid charity shop by the bus station. Yes, *that* one. I *know*, you don't have to say anything. . .

Love
Heather x

PS Thanks for your emails. But it would be really nice to meet up again – it seems like a long time since the café by the park.

**From:** **wombat**

**Subject:** **Me again**

**Date:** **Monday 23 April**

**To:** **rsmith@smiledentalgroup**

It's me again.

It's about 1.30 a.m. and I can't sleep. I just keep having this crazy thought over and over again.

And it's this (hang on to your seat!): how about – when you get yourself all properly settled, I mean – how about I come live with you?

See? Told you it was crazy!

What do you think?

Love

Your crazy daughter Heather x

# My Fairy Goth-mother

"'Never Gonna Give You Up', by Rick Astley."

"Really?" said Sylv, who was born on the 29th of August, 1987.

It was fun, having someone else's birthday Number One to look up. If Tiago hadn't been a stray with a mystery for a birthday, I'd have looked his up too. I'd sort of half-decided to give him a token birthday: 28th April, 2001, 'cause then he could have "Snoop Dogg" by Snoop Dogg.

"Wonder how it goes?" Sylv mused, as we strolled.

"Don't know; I was just about to download it when you turned up."

It was Friday evening and I didn't know how desperate I'd been to escape my room and the house until Sylv appeared like my Fairy Goth-mother (ha ha!) and whisked me off. Well, actually, she just told me she was taking Tiago out for last walk 'n' wee, and asked if I wanted to join them. (It turned out that Sylv wasn't allergic to *all* dogs, thank goodness – just sabre-toothed bull terriers, or perhaps just the people who owned them.)

Up until the moment when she'd knocked, I'd been hiding out upstairs from the crowd of dance buddies Mum had invited round to eat guacamole dip and practise some salsa. The trouble was, salsa was a very sexy sort of dance and seeing my mum doing some sexy dancing felt a bit wrong, like stumbling on your teacher buying diarrhoea tablets at the chemist's or something.

So I'd grabbed my jacket from the hall (now with lime-green walls, and chilli pepper fairy lights strung round the coat hooks) and snuck out with Sylv and Tiago before I had to witness any uncomfortable hip-swivelling.

Course, it wasn't just the hip-swivelling and salsa music I wanted to get away from; it was my computer too. I was getting sick of staring at my email in-box and willing Dad to get back to me. It had been four days now since I'd pinged my crazy idea over to him, and he'd obviously been so horrified by the idea that he couldn't bear to get back to me. And what was with his mobile? It always, *always* went to his message service whenever I tried it. (Though it might have helped to *leave* a message, I suppose. But I just got tongue-tied and mad and embarrassed the minute I heard that automated "...*after the beep*" voice.)

Still, never mind Dad being (very probably) horrified at my crazy idea; I was pretty horrified too. I'd been tired and mad at Mum for buying Tallie a dog when I'd never been allowed one, and mad too 'cause Mum had bought the boots I wanted in her new rock-chick mode, and 'cause she was going to take a dumb job that she'd probably hate.

At 1.30 a.m. that morning, I'd thought asking Dad if I could come and stay was a genius idea.

Course, that same genius idea that turned into the dumbest pile of *pants* in the world by 7.45 a.m. the next morning. . .

"By the way, does Jo-Jo actually live with us any more?"

It was a valid question for me to ask. I mean, I hardly ever saw my brother these days; now that his band stuff was out in the open – with our rock-chick Mum's blessing – Jo-Jo was on permanent manager duty. He'd zoom in from school, disappear into his room to zip through his homework, change into his indie gear and eyeliner, then blast his way out of the front door, pausing only to stuff whatever was for tea into an impromptu sandwich to eat on the move.

I was asking Sylv the question since she slept on the blow-up bed on his floor, and would know better than anyone if he was around.

"Sure, he does!" Sylv laughed.

She looked great tonight: full make-up and black lace-up corset worn over a maroon velvet dress. It was a bit much for a dog walk, specially since she was accessorizing it with a small, orange poop-scoop bag, but I was quite enjoying the stares from the regular dog-walkers and passers-by.

"Dad would ground him, if he was still at home," I told Sylv.

"Yeah, well, everything's changed for you guys." Sylv shrugged, turning into a leafy suburban street. "And that doesn't have to be a *bad* thing."

I thought about Mum and her sexy salsa and cool new haircut. I thought about Jo-Jo living his rock 'n' roll dream, while still keeping up his hobby of sabotaging Dad's stuff now and again (I spotted a pile of shoes in the bin the other day – every left shoe of Dad's that had been left behind in his wardrobe).

So change had turned them both marginally mad, but they were old enough to be responsible for their own madness.

"What about Tallie?" I said aloud, thinking about my kid sister, who was getting more and more eccentric by the minute. When I walked in on her in her bath tonight, she was busy blacking out *all* her teeth with those washable crayons you're meant to draw cute fish pictures with on the bath tiles or whatever.

"Tallie's great," said Sylv, who'd only known her as a sweetly strange, snaggle-haired, semi-feral five year old.

"She used to be totally different, though," I pointed out. "Tallie and Jo-Jo were *always* totally perfect, totally sorted. *I* was the only freaky one in the family."

God, Dad would hardly recognize three-quarters of his family now, I realized. Mum, his elegant wife; Tallie, his well-behaved pink princess; Jo-Jo, all ready to follow in his footsteps. Not any more.

"Hey, I know Jo-Jo couldn't stand all the pressure he felt to be 'perfect'," said Sylv, holding her fingers up to show the inverted commas (and accidentally strangling Tiago for a second by doing that). "So I guess in her own way, Tallie felt the same."

"You don't think she's going a bit, well, *loopy*, 'cause of Dad leaving?" I asked her.

"Course she is! You *all* are! It's only natural." Sylv laughed. "I just think Tallie is enjoying the freedom to be *stupid*. I mean, I went a little screwy too, but in the end I was really happy that way!"

"Screwy how?" I asked her.

Sylv stopped, and let her hands swoop theatrically

from her painted face to her Victoriana velvet dress.

"You didn't used to be a goth?" I asked, suddenly trying to imagine Sylv with a brown ponytail and freckles. It felt very wrong.

"My favourite colour used to be lilac, I helped out at a Brownie pack, I dreamed of playing Maria in *The Sound of Music*. What can I say? But I'm pretty sure I turned out to be a good person, so don't go worrying too much about Tallie yet."

Y'know, Sylv might look pretty weird, but *wow* was she smart and sensible underneath the black lipstick and corsets.

"Um, where are we going, exactly?" I asked, suddenly noticing that we'd ground to a halt outside a garage on a residential street I didn't know too well. Something very loud and guitar-based was booming out of the garage. If that was someone's car stereo, then they must have speakers the size of the windscreen.

"Staking out the bad boyfriend," Sylv admitted, shooting me a rueful smile, while she played with her broken heart necklace. "That's his house. They rehearse in his dad's garage."

Sylv – the well-balanced (goth) girl – was a *stalker*?

"But . . . why?" I asked, bending down to pat Tiago. He seemed reassuringly sane at the moment. I mean, inside his doggy head could be a whole pile of doggy madness (like something out of one of my daft, cut-out *Far Side* cartoons) but as he couldn't talk, I'd never know about them.

"Just 'cause someone stops loving you, it doesn't mean it's easy for you to stop loving *them*. . ."

So Sylv was having trouble locating her Loving Him Button, so she could switch it to "off". I guess I could relate to that.

"Omigod . . . the garage door's opening – we've got to get out of here!" Sylv muttered.

*Out* of here? What did she mean? Sylv had obviously got all dressed up, presumably in case her ex, Ade, spotted her lurking and fell madly in love with her all over again. And now she wanted to *run*?

Oops, I couldn't get any further into that thought tangle, 'cause of another tangle, this time involving my legs and Tiago's lead, as he tried to bolt after Sylv.

Add to that my mobile ringing, and life was getting *very* complicated.

"Hello?" I said breathlessly, once the three of us were safely hidden down a nearby alley. It was Mum calling; the screen had beamed up "Home" in the darkness.

"Hello, Heather?" said a tentative voice that was familiar, but certainly wasn't my mum's.

"Yes?" I replied, hearing the salsa music and voices still going strong in the background.

"This is Krystyna. I just tried to phone your brother, but he does not pick up."

The music was loud enough from outside here on the pavement; no way would Jo-Jo hear anything from inside Ade's rehearsal room/garage.

"What's up?" I asked, buffeted by a slight wave of panic. "Why were you trying to get hold of Jo-Jo?"

"Don't worry, nothing is badly wrong. But your mother is a little upset – I think it would be nice if you came home."

My mum always said I had an over-active imagination, and at Krystyna's words it went into hyper-drive straight away. I mean, what could've upset my mum? I ran through several possibilities at lightning speed, from the feasible (two), to the ridiculous (three).

1) Mum had suddenly found herself reminded of the break-up and got herself in a state
2) Mum had found out Dad had moved in with a gorgeous Russian pole-dancer
3) Mum had caught sight of her new haircut and decided she regretted it
4) Mum had looked at the lime-green walls in the hall and decided she regretted it
5) Mum had got drunk on sangria and snogged Tiago (the dance teacher, not the dog) and immediately regretted it

It turned out . . . ah, but that would be giving it away.

I'll just give a couple of little hints about the correct answer; she wasn't Russian, or a pole-dancer . . .

Dad –

I'm very confused. When you dropped your bombshell, you said there was no one else involved. Oops, that seems to have been a lie!

And when I saw you at the café and told you Jo-Jo suspected that wasn't true, you started to get all cross with me. *Not* fair, *at all*.

So anyway, I guess your new girlfriend is. . .

a)  the person you went running off to see when we were at the café
b)  the person you're living with now
c)  the reason why you obviously thought me moving in with you would be a terrible idea. So terrible, you didn't even bother to get back to me

Explanations, excuses, apologies would be nice.

Heather

PS I put that dried heather you gave me in the bin.
PPS That new aftershave that I think your new girlfriend gave you – it smells of cat wee.

# The Second Bombshell

Krystyna was still shooing well-meaning, sympathetic salsa-ers out of our front door when me, Sylv and Tiago got back, followed closely by Jo-Jo.

I'd called my brother the minute I'd got off the phone from Krystyna and told him what was going on. I'd called from the shame-saving safety of an alleyway around the corner from Ade's house, and – fingers crossed and hurray for good luck – he'd picked up during a lull between songs.

"What's going on?" I asked Krystyna in a panic, echoed by Jo-Jo's gruff voice, as he hurried down the path behind us.

"Your father, he has called," Krystyna said, with a shrug of her shoulders and a concerned frown on her face. "He has told your mother something. Please . . . you must go to her. You need to hear."

Dad.

Dad's dumb phone call.

Dad's dumb phone call, which I felt (urgh) partly responsible for.

Here's the chain of events (hey, there *had* to be one; even Dad wasn't dumb or mean or stupid enough to just pick up the phone and say "Hi, Joanna – how are you? By the way, I forgot to mention that I left you for another woman. Byeeee!").

And it went like this. . .

- Dad's email at work had been down for a few days.
- Dad's email gets fixed on Friday afternoon, and he picks mine from Monday – the one I wrote when I was seriously miffed with Mum for buying my tooth-free sister a dog, etc., etc., and asking to come stay with him (eek).
- As soon as Dad finishes up at work (which is late, as he has so much catching up to do after taking time off), he goes "home" (more on that in a second), and blasts off at Mum down the phone.
- Mum is caught off-guard, 'cause a) she hasn't had a conversation with Dad since he left, and b) she has a house full of people whooping along to sexy salsa music. She tells him he has a cheek to phone and have a go at her.
- Dad has a go back, telling her she's obviously not looking after us properly, as she's too busy turning the house into some kind of club.
- The two of them keep throwing angry words at each other, till Dad wins the bout hands down with a very low punch indeed. Let's call it the Second Bombshell. The Second Bombshell is called Nina. She is one of his patients.

"Oh."

That was Sylv, the first of us to speak, as Mum finished telling us her very sorry tale.

"Here," said Krystyna, bustling into the dishevelled party room (i.e. our living room), with a new box of tissues grabbed from somewhere, and offering it straight to a runny-nosed Mum.

"Are you OK?" I asked, feeling sad as I stared at my mum's now too-bright party top and somehow-limp flowery hair clip. She needed a hug straightaway if not sooner – and I was the girl for the job.

"She is OK. She has many excellent friends," said a stoic Krystyna, answering for Mum. "And good children also."

"I'll punch his whitened teeth out next time I see him. . ." muttered over-protective Good Child Number One, *very* darkly.

For a while no one knew what to say as we all thought, miserably, how Dad had lied to us. I was still brooding on the mystery phone call that had sent him dashing from the café five minutes into our reunion.

Dashing, no doubt, straight into the arms of – *urgh*.

But then as soon as we all talked some more and Jo-Jo calmed down, me and my brother slipped into this black humour thing that we just couldn't stop.

"It's obvious!" I'd said first, as everyone initially looked blankly at me. "This Nina was a patient, right?"

"Right. . ." Mum answered warily, dabbing at her red-rimmed eyes.

"Well, she *must* have fallen for Dad's face mask and safety goggles!"

It was stupid.

A stupid, idiotic comment to make.

But Jo-Jo got it. Actually, I knew by their faces that

both Sylv and Krystyna got it too, except that not being part of the direct family, they didn't feel able to join in the joking straight off.

"Yeah!" laughed Jo-Jo. "And *he* fell for her plaque and bad breath!"

Somehow, that was it; the bubble of misery was broken. Mum laughed out loud. (What a fantastic sound!)

The fooling around went on, and horribly on, till Mum and me and Jo-Jo and Sylv – and even smile-allergic Krystyna – were laughing like we'd never stop.

We even woke Tallie up, which was quite something, considering she'd slept through an entire salsa class taking place in our living room one hour before.

"What's going on?" she'd asked, appearing sleepily in the living-room door in her pyjamas, hugging Mr Boo. I noticed that dozy as she was, Tallie's voice had pretty much returned to normal now that she'd got used to her missing tooth.

"Nothing," I lied easily to my nicely-spoken little sis, before I dissolved into giggles.

I mean, *wow*, that "nothing" was *so* far from the truth. . .

And though the giggles had well and truly worn off by the time I emailed Dad, even the memory of them made me feel better.

Two days on from Dad's Second Bombshell.

To be exact, it was 10 a.m. on the morning of Sunday, 28th April.

It was Tiago's (token) birthday, and he was getting

breakfast in bed. Mum's bed. Which was actually a king-size, but felt a little snug with all of us (a mum, a dog, three "kids" and a goth) sprawled on it.

"'Tiago' – *that* would be a good name!" said Tallie, lying flat on her tummy, kicking her ankles in the air, and feeding beefy-smelling biscuits one-by-one to our delirious dog.

"I dunno." Jo-Jo shrugged. "It might make the band sound like they play Flamenco or something."

Apart from celebrating our pooch's honorary birthday, we were all trying to help a tired-looking Jo-Jo come up with a new name for his band. So far they'd been called Round Cube, which they all thought was kind of clever, till someone in the audience at a warm-up gig at the Coach and Horses had shouted out a much ruder-sounding version of their name that hadn't occurred to them before. ("You mean, 'Round Boo—'" Tallie had started to say, before Jo-Jo had slapped a hand round her mouth and threatened to force-feed her dog biscuits unless she shut up.)

So the name had to go. Jo-Jo and the boys had to think of something quick, before posters were printed for the big gig in the park coming up in just a few weeks' time.

"Mr Boo?" Tallie suggested hopefully, squashing a finger into the tummy of her even more punk'd teddy (he had ten safety pins in one ear alone).

"Sounds like someone who comes along to kiddy parties and makes balloon animals," said Sylv, lazing in her goth version of PJs, which consisted of black leggings and a T-shirt with pink skulls dotted on the sleeves.

I glanced warily at Tallie's teddy and thought about what Sylv had just said. If a human version of Mr Boo turned up at a kiddy party, all the parents would be grabbing their children to their bosoms and fleeing for the exits *tout suite*.

"*I* know!" said Jo-Jo, with a wicked grin on his face. "How about 'Bad Dad'!"

"Oh, shush! *Please!*" Mum groaned, chucking a pillow at him. But she was smiling, which was great. Friday night's Bombshell had dented her round the edges, but it was lovely to see she wasn't completely sunk in a pit of doom, or about to hibernate again.

"Well, since Bad Dad is too awful," I suggested, "how about Bad Boyfriend?"

I grinned straight at Sylv, who rolled her eyes and automatically rubbed her broken heart with her fingers.

"Catchy," nodded Jo-Jo, who still had traces of last night's eyeliner smudged around his lashes. "Might make my obnoxious but talented lead singer leave the band, though! Hey, what about that old nickname of yours, Heather?"

"Wombat?" I said, blushing at how truly dumb that sounded now he'd said it aloud. I'd *have* to change it.

"That *is* truly dumb," grinned Jo-Jo. "No, I meant that other one I thought you were going to use – what did I use to call you when I was a kid and you were a baby?"

"Scooter!" Mum laughed, which made Tallie immediately pull a big grin and show off her war wound.

"Scooter's not bad. . ." Jo-Jo mumbled thoughtfully.

"What about Pearl?" said Sylv, holding her hand under the necklace that I'd idly draped over my head this morning, as I bumbled around my room, planning on being ruthless and sorting out my mess, before I got distracted and started reading through a pile of two-year-old magazines I'd been about to chuck.

"Nah, Pearl's too weedy," said Jo-Jo.

"Excuse me!" Mum budged in. "You're maligning the name of your great-granny, who could *never* be described as 'weedy'!"

"No, Pearl was just *mad*, entering all those competitions to travel the world and then never going anywhere!" Jo-Jo laughed.

"Ah, but that was quite sad. That was all because of Joe, the one that got away," said Mum, pointing to the engagement ring around my neck.

"The ex-fiancé," I asked, intrigued to hear the story at last.

"The ex-fiancé." Mum nodded. "He was a Scottish engineer, and he headed off and spent his life working all over the world, building dams and bridges. Pearl was too scared to go with him – it felt like too big a step for a young girl, back in the 1930s. So they broke up, and she eventually met my grandad at a dance. But I think Pearl always regretted never seeing the world, and regretted never having the confidence to do it, even when she was older, after Grandad Jonny died."

"So do you think Pearl married your grandad on the rebound?" I asked.

"Oh, no! She loved her Jonny!" Mum said assuredly. "But her ex-fiancé always had a small, special place in her heart. Actually, I remember her once telling me that you can love lots of people in your life, but in different ways."

Silence.

I think for that one second, all of us piled on the bed were thinking about people we used to love, and maybe still did . . . or didn't. I don't think any of us could say for sure how we were feeling.

*"Uck-uck-uck . . . bleurrrrrrghhhhhhhhhh!!"*

I don't think it was the soppy story of Pearl and her long-lost sweetheart that got Tiago barfing – just too many doggy biscuits.

As everyone groaned and squirmed and tried to figure out how best to clean up the mess, my befuddled head switched from thoughts of Pearl's quirky love life to Dad's hidden affair.

Did he still love us, if he was busy loving "Nina" and her plaque and bad breath, I wondered?

The urge to never have anything to do with Dad again fought against my natural urge to see what "Nina" looked like, and how they were together.

Hey, maybe there was a way to get around both these urges.

Maybe I just needed stalking lessons from Sylv. . .

Hi Dad

I just picked up that email you sent yesterday morning. I hadn't turned on my computer for a couple of days, 'cause I wasn't too much in the mood to hear from you, as you probably sussed.

I guess I should say thanks for apologizing and being v. sorry your "news" all came out at the wrong time and in the wrong way and everything.

But one thing I got to thinking about: when you were trying to explain about your new girlfriend, you said, tough as it was, you knew "instinctively" that you HAD be with her, whatever happened.

Just remember it's tough on me (and Jo-Jo and Tallie), 'cause that means your "instincts" must've *also* been telling you that you HADN'T to be with us.

If you see what I mean.

I have to go.

Yours sincerely

Heather

PS Growing up, you used to tell us that the three important rules in our family were to a) look out for each other, b) tell the truth, and c) always brush our teeth.

I hope you're still brushing your teeth.

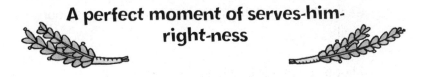

# A perfect moment of serves-him-right-ness

"Wait a minute . . . shouldn't we have gone to the doctor's first?" I said, slowing down as we trundled towards the Animal Aid shop.

"Why?" asked Jo-Jo.

"Well, don't we need inoculations before we go in there? Against yellow fever and malaria and whatever germs are in there?"

Sylv hit me gently on the arm.

"Come on, let's go see if your mum has survived the day. . ." she said, striding forward in her knee-high, black vinyl, lace-up boots.

"Me first!" shrieked Tallie, hurtling towards the shop at high speed on Jo-Jo's old scooter. A worried-looking old lady inside hauled the door open just in time to let Tallie screech inside.

"Wuff!" wuffed Tiago, coming out from behind a cloudy glass counter and wag-wagging his way towards us all.

"Ah, here they come!" said Mum brightly, as we all followed Tallie and filed in to the crowded interior. "My family, come to see how I'm doing!"

Mum was beaming. Maybe she'd had a much better time than I expected. Or maybe being delirious was the first sign of having contracted yellow fever. . .

"Guys, this is Betty and this is Jeannie, my sterling staff," Mum continued, holding her arms out in the direction of the two old ladies who were slipping on their jackets, in ready-to-go-home mode. "Ladies, let me introduce my family: this is my son, Jo-Jo, and his friend Sylv!"

Betty and Jeannie nodded and mumbled some wary hellos in the direction of my brother, resplendent in eyeliner, and Sylv, in all her goth grooviness.

"My little scooter girl here is Tallulah!" Mum said indulgently, while patting my sister on her crimson-streaked head.

(The crimson streaks – we'd all spent the May Day holiday yesterday painting more of the cream walls bright red, and Tallie had got most of the "brightness" in her hair.)

"Tallulah. What a . . . an *unusual* name," said Betty, picking her words carefully, if not truthfully. I mean, you didn't exactly need to be psychic to figure out that "fanciful" or "ridiculous" was more what she had in mind.

Meanwhile, Jeannie – the one who'd opened the door before Tallulah smashed headfirst into it – eyed up Tallie's choice of outfit today with barely disguised astonishment (pink sandals, pink socks, Jo-Jo's "I could, but I won't" T-shirt worn as a dress with a spangly Barbie belt, bat hair clips in her blonde/crimson tangled hair).

"And this is Heather!"

At my mother's words, the two ladies turned their attention to me . . . and immediately melted into warm smiles.

"Aren't you a lovely tall, slim girl!" cooed Betty. "You could have a model on your hands here, Joanna!"

Ho, ho, ho.

Yeah, *right* I could be a model. After the surprise of Jo-Jo, Sylv and Tallie, I think Betty was just so relieved to see a plain-ish girl in ordinary clothes that she got over-excitable and over-generous with the compliments.

"And Heather . . . what a beautiful name!" exclaimed Jeannie.

"Yes. It was a favourite of my gran's," said Mum.

What – my first name was influenced by Pearl too? I guess Mum might have got round to mentioning that when we'd all piled on the bed on Sunday, only the Pearl conversation got interrupted by the unexpected reappearance of those beefy chunks. . .

"Now what *is* that old Scottish song?" Jeannie suddenly muttered, looking questioningly at Betty. "The one about 'will ye go, lassie, go?'"

"*I* know!" said Betty. "'Wild Mountain Thyme'!"

And next thing, they were both off, singing their way through some sad-sounding folk thing, in those trilling, wibbly soprano voices that old ladies always use, oblivious to the fact that Tallie had now wandered off and put on a pair of red stilettos, Sylv was eyeing up a black silk dress on a rack, Jo-Jo was flipping through a box of old LPs and Tiago was mournfully howling along.

Only Mum and I were paying full attention; Mum, because these two women were her new employees, and me because as they seemed to be crooning in my honour, it would be rude not to. And in spite of everthing, their compliments *had* given me a little bit of a glow inside. Maybe, just maybe, I wasn't such a total wombat after all.

But while they crooned, I couldn't help thinking about the bus station opposite. Right there, I could catch the number thirty-eight bus, and it would take me all the way to Dad's surgery. As my stalking advisor, maybe I could get Sylv to come with me; I could sidle up to her in a few minutes' time, while Mum was making us a cup of tea in brown-stained mugs, or giving us a guided tour of the cobwebs or something.

Then again. . .

It's just that even though I'd confided in Sylv about my urge to spy on Dad, it didn't mean she'd make a particularly great spy-buddy. Having an extravagant goth by your side when you're trying to remain incognito would be like wandering around with a giant neon arrow above your head saying "I'M HERE!!".

It was OK for Sylv to live with the risk of getting spotted when she was stalking her bad boyfriend, but that was because she half-*wanted* him to catch her (just look how dressed up she was for Friday night's dog-walk if you want proof). "I suppose I'd love for him to see me and realize he's made a terrible mistake," she'd said wistfully, when we were busy doing our bank holiday paint-fest. But I dunno. Having someone sit for hours, or maybe days or weeks working out the lyrics of a song where they chuck you didn't sound like a *whim* to me. . .

"Fantastic! Really lovely, ladies!" Mum said, clapping as Betty and Jeannie came to the end of their mournful lament. It was a cue for me to start clapping feebly too, and mumble a slightly embarrassed thanks.

"Now then!" said Mum, as soon as she'd ushered the ladies on their way, and closed the shop door. "Welcome to my empire! Where will I start? Slightly grubby clothes? Or very dusty ornaments!!"

At least she had a sense of humour about it. And since she was in such a good mood, she wouldn't miss little old me.

"Actually, I've got to go, Mum. Becca invited me for tea, if that's all right, and we've got to do some project thing together first," I lied. It was worryingly easy, now that I'd had so much practice (or maybe I'd just caught the lying bug from Dad).

"Ah, what a pity – I was going to let you loose with one of these!" Mum laughed, holding out a multi-coloured feather duster.

"See you later," I said, hurrying out of the door, scratching at myself and wondering if it was possible to pick up fleas that fast. . .

Stupid-but-interesting fact Number One: dentures were once made out of hippopotamus teeth.

Stupid-but-interesting fact Number Two: sharks grow a new set of teeth every two weeks.

Stupid-but-interesting fact Number Three: hardcore goths can get crowns made for their teeth in the shape of fangs (no prizes for guessing who told me *that*).

Y'know, I think I was frightening the newsagent.

He probably thought I was acting all agitated because I was working myself up to steal the takings of his till or a box of Mars Bars or something. I could imagine how I looked: holding a magazine open in front of me which

I blatantly wasn't reading, rubbing agitatedly at my nose, and mumbling stupid-but-interesting facts to myself to calm my high-speed heart rate.

I checked my kitten-face watch for the seventy-fifth time this minute. Wow, this spying business was nerve-shredding. But it should soon be over; even from here, in a shop on the opposite side of the road, I could see the top of Dad's head above the half-blinds screening the surgery windows, which meant he was in clear-up mode.

My plan?

Well, my plan was rubbish, but I didn't know what else to do.

Here it was (no sniggering): Dad would leave, get in his car, and I would follow him. On the scooter I'd borrowed from Tallie (she'd made me promise to paint her toenails purple in exchange).

In case you didn't get that: I was going to follow my dad in his Audi on a *kids' scooter*. No, I didn't see how I was going to do it either, but my excuse was that in the five weeks since The Bombshell, my rickety brain was just that little bit more rickety, like a wooden rope bridge with a few crucial planks missing.

And then, ah!

I held by breath for far too long, same as Becca does when she sees Jo-Jo. Dad's head had vanished, which meant he'd be out in the reception area, setting the alarm and getting ready to leave. I stood on my tiptoes to check that my getaway vehicle was still leaning against the window there, and hadn't been nicked by any joy-riding seven-year-olds.

There he was! Closing the white door behind him,

he'd turn and *bleep-bleep* his car keys at the Audi any second now and I'd have to zoom out of here at high speed and fol—

Oh.

No *bleep-bleep*.

No Audi.

Just a smile in the direction of a pretty woman with long red hair, who'd just climbed out of a VW Golf to meet him.

Nina.

My heart and my legs turned to the consistency of lumpy custard.

Weird – this Nina person didn't look exactly pleased to see *Dad*, though.

She took a few steps towards him and *oops!*

*Yuck!*

Now she seemed to be doing an impersonation of Tiago on Mum's bed the other day – she'd barfed right over Dad's shoes!

*How romantic...* I thought to myself, relishing the perfect moment of serves-him-right-ness in the midst of my general nervousness.

With butterflies battering around in my tummy, I carried on watching as Dad leant Nina up against the car, then began rubbing her back as he chatted to her with a concerned look on his face. Opening the passenger door, he gently helped her inside as if she was made of something very delicate and precious, not a person who smelled of vomit. Next, he hurried around to the other side – with only a brief pause to shake each foot – and slid himself into the driver's seat.

I felt very strange all of a sudden – like I was seasick or something. Maybe I was about to barf too. But before I could, in the next nanosecond, Dad (and Nina) had raced off in a squeal of tyres.

Racing or not, I wouldn't have been able to follow my dad on the scooter if I'd wanted to; my legs were shaking too much.

"Are you going to buy that magazine, or what?" the nervous newsagent bellowed at me.

I guessed I'd better. I didn't really *want* a copy of *Antiques Today*, but I could hardly just shove it back on the shelf, not when I'd been nervously biting on the top of the pages. . .

Hi Dad

Just got in and picked up the email you must have
sent during your lunch hour or whatever.

Anyway, yes thanks, the rest of the bank holiday
weekend went really well. We spent yesterday
painting the kitchen pink and purple and Mum's
room crimson. They look really great, specially with
all the new prints and pictures Mum's put on the
walls. Tallie got carried away and ended up painting
the holly bush outside, and most of herself by
accident.

We all had a really great laugh. We really did.

We're all really fine.

Mum started her new job today and is loving it.
The shop's not as bad as I thought, in fact it's full of
very interesting stuff.

I have to go now.

Heather

## The Bad Boyfriend voodoo doll

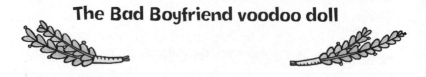

Hey, everyone needs a hobby; Sylv's just happened to be stalking.

She was doing a little light stalking this Saturday morning, with me, Becca and Tallie keeping her company, since none of us had anything better to do. Certainly not now that Tallie had decided ballet was "too pink and tinkly" and given up her classes.

Jo-Jo had a new hobby too – helping Mum at the charity shop. Not so much out of the kindness of his heart and his love for lickle animals, oh no. It was because he'd decided to take driving lessons, so the band could get a van, so that Scooter (yep, that's the name they'd all settled on) could properly go on tour. His version of helping out at Mum's shop was scouring for anything remotely interesting, selling it on eBay, and splitting the takings with Mum (well, Mum's *till*, strictly speaking). His share paid for driving lessons.

So Animal Aid was where my brother – the entrepreneur – was hanging out this morning. We, meanwhile, were in Fantastic Gadgets in the shopping centre, which just *happened* to be across the concourse from HMV, into which a certain lead singer had just ambled. I'd been really intrigued to see Ade at last, to see this rock god that Sylv couldn't get out of her head or heart, but he was kind of a disappointment. He looked like every indie boy I'd ever seen: skinny-ish and more importantly *floppy,* from his hair to his baggy T-shirt to his low-slung jeans.

Still, if Floppy Ade happened to look round right now, he probably wouldn't have been able to spot Sylv, her cover was so good. She was positioned right behind some poor sales assistant from Fantastic Gadgets, who'd been forced into wearing a blow-up sumo wrestler suit to hand out flyers to passers-by.

"Hey, how do you make this stop?" Tallie asked, as a furry robot guinea pig followed her around the shop, squeaking at her.

I think it was meant to be cute, but it was actually a tiny bit menacing.

"I don't know – go over and check the instructions on the box," I suggested.

Y'know, I think I needed an instruction manual for *my brain.* I needed to locate the batteries so I could take them out, so I wouldn't have to keep watching re-runs of Dad and the barfing Nina playing in my head over and over again. For two weeks now, I hadn't been able to shift the thought of how kind and concerned he'd been with her, when only a few days before he'd been the exact *opposite* to Mum on the phone.

Yep, it had been a whole two weeks since I'd come home (on Jo-Jo's stupid old scooter, with my stupid copy of *Antiques Today*) and sent Dad the email where I'd tried to make out that we were all doing *fabulously* well without him, in the hope that it might twist the knife into his happy heart. I didn't let on that I'd seen him.

And the messages Dad sent *me* in the last fortnight?

Well, they were generally all grovelling, all trying to explain how much he still loved us, how complicated everything was (more than I knew, he said), how upsetting it was that loving one particular person meant hurting others.

I'd mostly ignored them, answering only a couple, both times saying I was too busy to get back to him properly. Truth was, I was so cross with Dad that the only thing I felt like writing was ARRRRRGGGGHHHHHH!! in giant letters, all fiery red.

"Isn't that your phone?" asked Becca, pointing at my bleeping bag.

"Mmm. Probably Dad again," I replied, pretending to look at stuff on the nearest shelf and pretending I didn't care.

"Why don't you just answer him?"

I shrugged a casual dunno. Mainly because I didn't really know *what* I thought exactly.

"It's complicated," I said, repeating Dad's phrase when I realized that Becca wasn't going to let me away with a simple shrug.

At the same time, I idly picked something off the shelf and began playing with it.

*Burppppppp!!*

Becca took the unexpectedly rude novelty bottle opener out of my hand and put it back on the shelf.

"You can't keep ignoring your dad!" she said, almost sternly. "If you're so angry with him, why don't you just tell him?"

"Don't want to," I muttered, knowing I sounded about three.

"So it's better just to *mope* and *moan* all the time? Yeah, that's a *really* good idea! *That'll* show him!" Becca almost snapped at me.

I wasn't used to Becca being stern or snappy.

It's not that I didn't completely understand her frustration with me – I mean, she'd had to listen to me droning on and on about the Dad situation for the last couple of months – but I was feeling kind of dumb and confused right now and wanted her to stop.

"Don't move!! Don't say another word – or I'll shoot!" I yelped, grabbing a marshmallow catapult off the shelf and pointing it right at her.

Becca rolled her eyes and folded her arms across her chest, giving in to my goofing with a pretend huff.

"How cool is this thing?" I said, studying the contraption I was holding. Think how different war would be, if soldiers and rebel forces were issued with marshmallow catapults instead of AK47s. It would be very handy in marriage breakdowns too; instead of parents hurling accusations at each other, they could just blast one another with soft, squidgy sweets. Excellent.

"Look, I just think you should talk to your dad, or text him or something, and let him know how mad you are with him for not telling you the truth about Nina," said Becca, sounding very wise and grown-up and not her usual nice-but-clunky self at all.

*She should write an advice column in a magazine when she's older*, I thought to myself, as I half-noticed Tallie having her head clunked by some shopper's big shoulder bag.

157

"Mum said it's not good to bottle up your feelings. . ."

Aha! So Becca had been blabbing all to her mother again! She really couldn't help it. Next thing, Mrs Fitzgerald would be organizing family counselling for us all.

"Listen – I'm going to do something!" said Sylv, swooping suddenly towards us in a flap of her floor-length purple rubber skirt. Her pale blue eyes twinkled with some amazing, slightly edgy plan.

"What?" I asked, lowering my catapult.

"I'm going to go for a coffee!"

Out of the corner of my eye, I could see Becca's face scrunch into a puzzled "Huh?".

"Um. . . OK," I shrugged, knowing there had to be more to it than the need for a caffeine rush.

"Ade likes to go to the café in here and read his music mags once he buys them," Sylv began to explain.

She was oblivious to the stare of the sumo wrestler, who'd seen plenty of weird things in the shop, but none as spectacularly weird as Sylv. (Ha – he should try taking a look in the *mirror*.)

"I usually just watch him from behind a pillar," Sylv continued. "but today I think I'll get there before him, and pretend to be flicking through a magazine myself, and see what happens."

It sounded like a useless plan. *Nothing* would happen. Ade would probably take one look at Sylv and slope off, unseen. But considering *I* was the girl who'd planned on following my dad's high-speed car on a kiddy scooter not so long ago, I could hardly talk.

"Sounds good," I lied. "Do you want us to come along

and meet you after Tallie's finished playing here? We could sit at another table. . ."

"Yes – definitely!" said Sylv, turning to leave in a flapping whirl of black and purple. "Wish me luck!"

The sumo took a step back, as if he was worried Sylv might lean over and stick her fangs in his inflatable neck.

"Good luck!" I called after her, knowing she'd need a truck-load. She'd probably need a whole pile of sympathy too, when her useless plan backfired (just like she'd had to comfort me with kind words and gloomy goth music when I'd come back from spotting Dad and his girly together).

*Maybe I could get Sylv a little present*, I suddenly decided, glancing around me. I didn't suppose she'd particularly want a marshmallow catapult or a burping bottle opener. . .

But she *might* want a Bad Boyfriend Voodoo Doll!

"What's that?" asked Becca, as I hurried over to the till.

"She can call it Ade and stick pins in it!" I explained, holding up the squashy, shapeless, sort of *floppy* toy. It had slogans all over it, like "Never calls" and "Flirts with your friends". Sadly, it didn't have "Chucks you publicly in a song", but it was as close as I could get.

"Pity there's not a Bad Dad one," said Becca, her arms still crossed defensively across her chest.

I gave a wry smile to show I got the joke, paid for my pressie, and shouted for Tallie to come.

From nowhere, she popped up by my side like a Jill-in-the-box. She was giggling, for no specific reason I could see.

I found this more than slightly unnerving.

"What's so funny?" I asked, as we all walked out of the shop.

"Nothing! Hee, hee, hee!"

I looked at Becca, over the top of Tallie's head. Becca looked at me and frowned.

"Are you sure?" I double-checked, giving Tallie a second chance to own up to whatever little mischief had got her giggling so much.

"I didn't do *anything*! Much. Well, there's this *one* thing that's just *so* funny. . ."

We didn't get to hear what was "*so* funny", because of the racket going on behind us. The security alarm had gone off at the doorway of Fantastic Gadgets, and the guard was now hauling an embarrassed-looking woman back to the shop. The woman who'd thunked Tallie over the head with her bag and never stopped to say sorry. She was protesting her innocence, demanding to know what she was supposed to have done.

"Hee, hee, hee!" giggled Tallie.

"Oh, God, *look*!" gasped Becca. "At that woman's bag, I mean!"

I looked.

I saw.

Peeking out of the woman's big, slouchy shoulder bag was a small, furry face. It was squeaking.

Urgh. I had a funny feeling I knew who'd put that robot guinea pig in there. . .

**From:** wombat

**Subject:** Shoplifting-by-proxy

**Date:** Saturday 12 May

**To:** rsmith@smiledentalgroup

Dad –

I know you tried to get me on my mobile this morning, but I was kind of busy, trying to make sure Tallie wasn't *arrested*, if you're interested.

She did this dumb thing where she shoplifted-by-proxy (that's when you use someone else to do something, Sylv says). She put a guinea pig (not a real one) in a woman's bag, and the woman got caught with it, and I took Tallie back to explain and apologize. The security guard and the shop manager and the woman all went ballistic with *me*, which was amazingly not fun.

Becca says her mum says that Tallie is probably acting weird like this as a reaction to you going.

But don't panic about Tallie – *Mum* sorted it out.

She had this big chat with her and Tallie knows what she did was wrong. She's in her room right now, writing a letter of apology. She got Jo-Jo to take a photo of her looking sad and is sticking it on the letter to show she's genuine.

Just thought you should know.

Heather

## 17 years good – 1 bad thing = zero

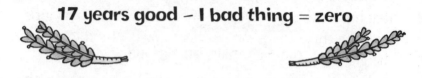

*Sighhhhhh* . . . THUD!!

That was the sound of scores of girls seeing my brother and immediately fainting from longing.

OK, so I'm exaggerating, but not much. Standing outside the school gate with my brother was a pretty fascinating experience. Some girls blatantly stared or smiled his way, putting an extra sway in their walk or muttering smirked whatevers with their equally smirking mates. Some girls got giddy the way Becca did, caught out by Jo-Jo's gorgeousness, blushing or forgetting to breathe, as if they'd turned a corner and walked slap-bang into the magical, twinkling world of Narnia.

Jo-Jo, of course, was – very sweetly – blind to it all. Slouching with his hands in his jeans pockets, he was lost in some musical netherworld, his head grooving back and forth in time to whatever was blasting from his i-Pod.

"Let me hear," I said, more in sign language than out loud.

While we were waiting for Mum to pick us up and give us a lift home from school, I decided I might as well have some entertainment, apart from people-watching Jo-Jo's admirers.

My brother unplugged himself and graciously handed over his tiny white headphones.

"What are you listening to?"

"Scooter," he said, doing his arm stretch thing now that his hands were free and unconsciously causing girls within a three-kilometre radius to *melt*. "It's the set for the gig in the park."

"Which is happening when, again?" I checked with him.

"A week on Saturday. You coming?"

He said it so casually, but I certainly didn't *feel* casual.

Wow, I'd never been to a gig before. Around our way, bands only ever played in clubs you had to be at least eighteen to get in. Call me dumb, but it had never occurred to me that I could just hang out and watch a bunch of bands in the park with Becca, and Sylv if she was up for it.

Ha, ha, ha . . . of *course*, Sylv would be up for it, since it involved staring at the ex-Bad Boyfriend uninterrupted. She needed her fix of Ade, having seen nothing of him at the café on Saturday (didn't I say he'd spot her and scarper?).

"Yeah, of course I'm coming." I replied to Jo-Jo's question with a shrug, sounding cool but feeling as chilled as a newly made jelly inside. "Guess I better find out what they sound like, though!"

I slipped the headphones in my ears, muttering a silent "*Yes!!*" of excitement to myself, and tuned into the track that was playing. The music sounded good, in a raw, loud, grannies-would-hate-it way.

And then I sussed out what I was actually listening to.

"*. . .So, sorry, Sylvia, but me and you are through.*

*So, sorry, Sylvia, it's not me, it's you. . ."'*

I whipped the headphones off as if they'd burnt me.

"What?" said Jo-Jo.

"How can you listen to that Ade guy sing that song? How can you listen to him dumping your friend like that?" I asked.

"Hey, I had a real go at him when I first heard it," Jo-Jo replied. "But then we decided we had to be professional about it."

"What d'you mean?"

"Well, as the manager of the band, I've got no say in what songs the guys decide to perform, and as the singer in the band, Ade has got no right to make any comments about my private life, like the fact that Sylv is my mate and is staying at our place. We just steer clear of the subject and get on with our jobs."

Jo-Jo sounded very mature all of a sudden. Pity he wasn't as mature in *every* aspect of his life.

"I saw Sylv's Bad Boyfriend voodoo doll on the floor of your room this morning," I mentioned.

The Bad Boyfriend voodoo doll – full of pins – was looking a little different from when I bought it on Saturday. It had a new face attached to it, for instance.

"Oh, yeah!" Jo-Jo laughed (sending shivers up the spines of his passing girly fans).

He'd obviously found a "good" use for Dad's head, after cutting it out of the holiday snap on the pinboard the other week. Maybe Jo-Jo's time would've been better spent revising for his upcoming exams, instead of doing bad karma handicrafts.

"D'you think you'll ever forgive Dad?" I heard myself asking, out of the blue.

Me? I wasn't sure how I'd answer that, if it was the other way around. I wasn't sure what Mum would say to that question either, only I know she seemed to be coming out from under a dark cloud (a dark *duvet*, in the early days), and that could only be good.

But Jo-Jo?

I couldn't help wondering if this was the point where I should tell my brother about all the emails that had zapped back and forth between me and our absent-without-leave father. Maybe confess that I'd seen him twice, even if one time was just for a few minutes face-to-face, and the other time was in spy mode. . .

"What do *you* think, Heather?" said Jo-Jo, his voice all gravelly with sarcasm.

Well, that was the trouble; I hadn't a *clue* what to think. I had such a jumble of thoughts going on at any one time that my brain was asking me to pay it overtime. I mean, even though I'd been trying to keep my dad at bay for the last while, the sad, sorry stuff he'd been saying in his emails and messages about love; about loving Nina, and loving us – and hating to hurt us at the same time – had been seeping into my head like maple syrup on to pancakes. Especially the last one, when he'd got back to me about Tallie and the shoplifting-by-proxy thing. Becca had told me to let him know how mad I was, but then he sounded so upset I began to feel squirms of guilt in between the blasts of rage. . .

If I read about this situation in a book, if the main character wasn't my dad and the people being hurt weren't me, Mum, Jo-Jo and Tallie, then I'd be swept up the sweet, sweet tragedy of it all, I really would. . . . Crazy, isn't it?

Here's another thought that had snuck into my head: last night I'd been staring at my shelves of rescue soft toys and realized that for every one that was genuinely lost, there was another that had been deliberately dumped. Some fluffy bunny might have done years of loyal hugging duty, only to be chucked away when one of its glued-on plastic eyes fell off.

Which got me thinking about Dad again. I mean, he hadn't had anything fall off; it's just that he'd been a pretty good parent for as long as Jo-Jo and me and Tallie had been alive and kicking. And then he goes and does something "bad" all of a sudden – but does that one "bad" thing wipe out all the good stuff?

[Formula: 17 years good – 1 bad thing = zero]

And once I'd got thinking about it, I'd had to admit to myself that there'd been plenty of Good Dad stuff. I'd snuggled down under my duvet and thought of a list –

- Dad always letting us win at games like Connect 4 all the time
- Dad cheering us on the first time any of us cycled with no stabilizers
- Dad teaching us to dive from the second highest board
- Dad and all of us watching the *Blue Planet* box set together
- Dad letting us (try to) chop logs in the holiday cottage we went to in Cornwall

- Dad filming every school show we were in and methodically editing it on the computer
- Dad teaching me and Jo-Jo to work i-Tunes

– until I fell asleep, and woke up this morning with my bedside light still on and the imprint of the book I'd been planning to read down the left-hand side of my face.

"What's your favourite memory of Dad?" I asked Jo-Jo now, hoping to dent a sentimental hole in his veneer of hate.

"Him leaving. With his suitcase. '*See* ya!'"

All this bolshy stuff was starting to exasperate me, if you want to know the truth. It was like he'd got himself so stuck in angry mode that he couldn't allow himself to think anything other than "AAAAAARGGHHHH!" when it came to our dad. Me? I bounced around between angry and forgiving, upset and sympathetic, which was totally exhausting but maybe a bit more realistic.

*PARPPPPPPPP!!*

*Oh, for goodness' sake*, I thought, picking up my school (plastic) bag and shuffling back on the pavement a couple of steps, out of the way of the terrible and thoughtless driver reversing badly into the parking space right in front of us.

*PARRPPPP-PAARRRPPP-PAAAAAARRRRRPPPP!!*

Now I was ready to get as angry and intolerant as Jo-Jo. The driver of this horrible, rusty old minibus/camper van thing was deafening me with his horn.

"What's this guy's prob—"

"Hey!!" Jo-Jo roared, interrupting me.

"HIYAAAAAAA!!" yelped Tallie, scrambling over

Mum's lap, along with Tiago, to lean out of the driver's side window. She was treating us to a full-beam, missing-toothed grin.

"Mum?"

I said that in a really teeny-tiny shocked voice.

Where was our flashy 4x4?

"Jump in!" Mum ordered brightly. "You need to tug really hard at the door, but it slides open OK if you do it right!"

I let Jo-Jo do the tugging, and after a minute or two of groaning and laughing (Jo-Jo both times – I was too stunned to make any noise at all), we were both inside a strange little world of old-fashioned chequered car seats and vats of empty space.

All my brain could think of was, Why, why, why, why. . .?

In fact it was so busy wondering Why, why, why, why? that I didn't realize Mum had started to explain till she was halfway through a sentence.

" . . .more room for picking up bags of donations for the shop. And then when Jo-Jo learns to drive, he can borrow it to drive the band to gigs."

"Wicked!!" gasped Jo-Jo, hardly believing his luck,

I could hardly believe what I was sitting in. It's not that I *liked* the 4x4, but I knew it cost a lot. Like, a *lot* – Dad was always going on about how much it was, even though he never said how much exactly, *and* he chose it for Mum to drive us around in the first place.

Whereas *this* . . . this must have cost about £2.50.

"Mum. . .?" I muttered in that teeny-tiny shocked voice again.

"It gets better, Heather!" said Mum, pulling the keys out of the ignition and waggling them at me. "Check this out!"

I didn't get it: she'd swapped the 4x4 for a rusty can on wheels and a very strange-looking keyring with a small cactus, a heart and a scarf that said "Mexico" dangling from it?

OK . . . if anyone wanted to translate, then that would be very nice, thank you, 'cause I hadn't a clue what was happening.

"I sold the car," said Mum, clocking my blank expression.

"I got that bit," I replied.

"And I bought this, because it was more practical."

"Uh-huh," I mumbled, following her flawed logic so far.

"And *this* is a clue to what I did with the rest of the money!"

I glowered again at the green, white and red keyring she was dangling and tried to figure it out. Had Mum shoved the extra wodges of cash that she's made in that box under my bed that said "Keyrings – keep out"? There was plenty of room for banded-up banknotes in there, since my keyring collection never got beyond the fingers of one hand.

"We're going on holiday to Mexico in the summer!" Tallie shrieked, unable to stand the suspense and my stupidity any longer.

"Wuff!" barked Tiago, leaping from the front seats to the back, where me and Jo-Jo were perched.

"You're kidding!" gasped Jo-Jo, which was nice, 'cause

I couldn't manage to talk.

"Absolutely not!" Mum beamed. "Me and your dad went there when we were travelling the world, and I'd love to take you guys! Let's fiesta, let's splash in the Pacific, let's dance. . ."

"Let's get kidnapped?" I suggested, remembering the scare stories I'd heard.

"That's only a risk in certain *South* American countries, honey," Mum said in a reassuring voice. "Mexico is in *Central* America."

Maybe I should concentrate on geography more.

But I couldn't concentrate on anything because I was suffering from a bad case of *inverse* déjà vu. Déjà vu is that sensation that you've been through the same situation before. *Inverse* déjà vu is a medical term I'd just invented for feeling like I didn't know *where* I was.

I mean, I was sitting in a strange vehicle, with a rock-chick mum, an eyeliner-wearing brother, a drooling dog, and a kid sister with crimson paint in her hair and, for some bizarre reason, a dog collar round her neck.

Was this really my once-upon-a-time perfect family? They didn't look anything like that holiday photo on the pinboard in the kitchen.

"Woof!" said Tallie.

My feelings exactly. . .

**From:** wombat

**Subject:** Woof

**Date:** Monday 14 May

**To:** rsmith@smiledentalgroup


Hi Dad

How are you?
  I'm OK.
  Tallie got into more trouble today, sort of. She wanted to take Tiago to show-and-tell at school, but Mum said no. So she took Tiago's collar in instead, which was fine, except she insisted on wearing it, and would only answer Miss de Rossi's questions with one bark for yes and two barks for no.
I'm a bit tired, so that's all for now.
  Love
  Heather x

PS Mum's got a new car/van/thing.

From:    **wombat**

Subject: **Me again**

Date:    **Monday 14 May**

To:      **rsmith@smiledentalgroup**


By the way, the stuff you've said about you being really in love with Nina and everything . . . I think I might be pleased for you. But it might take a little while.

OK?

Love

Heather x

# In the mood for dullness

Some statistics for you. It was:

- Eight weeks since The Bombshell
- Seven weeks till we left for our family (minus Dad) holiday to Mexico
- Two weeks till Sylv went to Camp America
- Four days till the gig in the park
- Two days since I'd last heard from Dad
- An hour since I got home from school
- Forty-five minutes since Jo-Jo stuck his music on really, really loud
- Thirty minutes since Tiago started barking in the garden, with Tallie shrieking along as they played chase
- Twenty minutes since Mum and Krystyna came through the door with shopping bags and put very loud salsa music on in the living room
- Ten minutes since Sylv went into the shower and started singing something about a Hong Kong garden at the top of her voice
- And a whole minute ago since I phoned Becca and asked (OK, begged) to come to tea at her place

"I've got to get out of this madhouse!" I'd told her,

moving a tail-less fluffy horse away from my ear so I could hear her better.

"Well, come on round to the dull house!" she'd joked, not realizing she was talking to a crazy girl submerged in soft toys at the time.

But forget the crazy thing for a second: oh *boy*, was I in the mood for a bit of dullness. Who'd've ever thought that I used to feel like the non-perfect, ditzy one in my family? Now I felt too stupidly normal compared to my salsa-ing mother, eyeliner-wearing brother and wild-child little sis to fit in (hey, I could *never* win).

But, whatever – the mad house, mad family, mad *me* was all getting too much. As the noise rattled and hummed outside my bedroom door, I'd gathered all the rescue toys off my shelves and put them on the bed, then I lay down and scooped them over me, like you do with sand when you're a kid on the beach. By the time I'd finished, only my hands and my nose were sticking out. If anyone had walked in on me, they'd have called the insane police, and I couldn't have blamed them.

And lying there, under my comforting pile of "pets", I fantasized about the calm, tasteful, minimal flat that I imagined Dad and Nina sharing. Maybe they had a spare room. Now that a bit of time had passed, Dad might reconsider the idea of having one well-behaved daughter move in with him. I'd be very low maintenance. I could help out with the cleaning and shopping and stuff (I'd got used to doing that when Mum was hibernating). I wouldn't take any of my collections and clutter up the place; oh, no. I'd travel light, just bringing a few clothes, my school books, and maybe that purse Dad bought me, so I looked grateful.

See what I mean about going mad?

I *had* to get out.

Mum wouldn't miss me for tea, I decided, as I pattered down the stairs to the hall and grabbed my trainers. She still had the odd down day, but most of the time she was heading onward and upward, thinking up new money-making and publicity schemes for the charity shop (my one suggestion – a sponsored clean-a-thon), or faffing around decorating the house with old knick-knacks from her travelling days (dragged down from the loft), or hanging out with her best buddy Krystyna. Like she was doing right now.

"I'm going to Becca's for tea," I said, hopping into the kitchen on one leg, as I tugged my trainer on the other foot.

Mum and Krystyna were both dancing as they unpacked shopping bags. A wiggle-waggle here with some nachos, a shimmy-shimmy there with bottles of wine. Hmm . . . not your average milk-and-tins-of-beans supermarket-shop, then.

"Oh, OK, Heather!" said Mum brightly, a see-through packet of what looked like streamers in her hand. "By the way, tell Becca we're having a party on Saturday night, if she'd like to come!"

"Why?" I asked with a frown, nearly toppling over. "Why are we having a party, I mean?"

"Oh, no reason . . . or *every* reason!" Mum laughed.

I couldn't remember ever having a party at our house – Mum and Dad used to pull faces at the idea and say they didn't fancy cleaning crisp crumbs out of the carpet for months. If it was our birthdays, we had parties in hired halls, or just special days out at theme parks or whatever.

Maybe working in a dump like the Animal Aid shop had made her immune to mess. Maybe a few crumbs seemed like nothing compared to other people's donated grime.

"Your mother just wants to celebrate," Krystyna chipped in.

Actually, I wasn't sure I liked Krystyna chipping into the conversation, or butting into our family life, for that matter. I guess I kind of resented her being so at home here, when I certainly didn't feel that way at the moment.

"Celebrate what?" I said, knowing I sounded deliberately grumpy.

"Just . . . celebrate!" Mum said, throwing her arms out wide. (I had a quick glance over at the wine, to check that she hadn't been drinking any already. Nope. She was just high on life, then.)

"Right, I'm off," I said, turning to leave.

"Hey, Heather!" Krystyna called after me, stopping me in my tracks.

"What?" I said, knowing I sounded like a sulky teenager.

"Catch!"

Something flew through the air, from Krystyna's hand to mine.

"I found it in the place they keep the trolleys at the supermarket. I thought you might like it."

A small, manky, stripy tiger with a smile but no nose gazed up imploringly at me.

"Thanks," I mumbled.

That sensation of being annoyed with someone and grateful to them at the same time: it feels a bit like indigestion, if you want to know. . .

*Tick-tock, tick-tock, tick-tock* went the clock on the wall of the dining room. You could hear it in the near silence of Becca's house. You wouldn't be able to hear Big Ben chiming in our place, it was so noisy.

"More potatoes, Heather?" asked Mrs Fitzgerald, hovering over me.

"No thank you," I replied.

*Clink-clunk, ker-chunk* went the clatter of knives and forks on the plates.

"So, how're your brother's exams coming along?" asked Mr Fitzgerald.

God, Jo-Jo's exams. I'd temporarily forgotten he was doing those. He didn't seem stressed, so that meant he'd be skimming through them, like he always did.

"Fine, I think." I nodded.

"Rebecca was telling us that you girls are off to a show on Saturday afternoon, to watch this band your brother is involved with!" said Mrs Fitzgerald, putting the potatoes down and settling back into her seat.

"Mmm, yeah," I answered her, through a mouthful of mashed potatoes.

"Your mother must be a little concerned that he's so interested in this pop group, though," Mrs Fitzgerald added. "It might interfere with his studies. And it's such a *shame* that he's given up his squash club, he was so good at it, wasn't he?"

*Tick-tock, tick-tock, tick-tock* went the clock on the wall, as I pretended my mouth was too full to answer her.

"Still, you're mother's probably quite busy with her new job," Mrs Fitzgerald carried on, as she clunk-clinked her cutlery. "*And* her busy social life. How is she enjoying . . . what's it called . . . 'salsa'?"

Great, Becca had been blabbing to her parents again. You could see where she got it from; the saying clunky things trait, I mean. At least Becca only came out with dumb, clunky comments, unlike her mum, who had a real talent for getting digs in under the guise of chit-chat. Just now, she'd said the word salsa like it was Spanish for *poo*. I think she'd prefered to think of my mum as the miserable, tragic, spurned wife than someone who could move on and grab a little fun out of life. I suddenly felt a huge surge of pride in my mother.

"Um, Heather says there's a party happening at their house on Saturday night," Becca barged in, trying for a change of direction for the conversation. "It's OK if I go, right?"

"Well, yes. . ." said Mrs Fitzgerald warily, looking slightly kerfuffled now that her interrogation of me had been foiled. Or maybe she was just kerfuffled at the idea of her daughter hanging out at a wild salsa den, or whatever she imagined our house had been transformed into.

*Tick-tock, tick-tock, tick-tock.*
*Clink, clunk, clatter.*

"Lovely sausages, dear," Mr Fitzgerald said to his wife.

"Mmm," murmured Mrs Fitzgerald.

Like a speeded-up film, I wolfed down as much of my tea as I could manage.

"Listen, I'm sorry, but I have to go. . . I forgot that I'd promised to babysit Tallie tonight and I didn't realize the time," I lied, glancing up at the tick-tocking clock.

I'm fickle, I really am. But I'd had enough of dull.

Bring on the salsa and the fun. . .

**From:** wombat

**Subject:** Welcome, number fifty-two!

**Date:** Tuesday 22 May

**To:** rsmith@smiledentalgroup

Hi Dad

I've just got number fifty-two in my rescued soft toy collection – Krystyna found him for me. He's a kind of cute tiger, only with no nose (how does he smell? Awful! Boom, boom!!).

Do you know a song called "Hong Kong Garden"? Sylv was singing it earlier in the shower. I just looked it up in the *British Book of Hit Singles*, and it's another Siouxsie and the Banshees track, and it got to Number Seven in 1978.

What stuff are you listening to at Nina's place? All your CDs are here. Why don't you come and collect them sometime? Only not Saturday night, 'cause Mum's having a party.

I'd invite you, but it might be too weird.

Love

Heather x

PS I started looking for stupid song titles at the *back* of the *British Book of Hit Singles* (just 'cause I hadn't found many stupid ones in the middle letters of the alphabet), and under "Z" there was "Zip-a-dee-doo-dah". I guess that is a dumb title, but the song's kind of sweet, since it's all about being happy.

Do you remember singing it to us when we were little? I do. But then you also sang "Shaddap You Face" when we were being too noisy (wow, that was a rubbish but kind of funny song).

# The tears of a goth

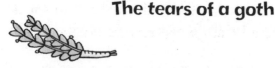

The St John's Ambulance Brigade, if you didn't know, are first aid experts who are at every big public show or whatever, in case people faint or choke on a hotdog or something.

They wear a sort of very proper uniform so that people can spot them easily. I peeked over the heads of the crowds lolling on the grass and spotted a couple of them standing outside their first aid tent, gazing around the park and probably wondering who their first patient might be.

Well, I might be able to help them out there. The guys from Scooter – helped by Jo-Jo – were just setting up their gear on stage, almost ready to begin their opening act set, and Becca and Sylv had stopped breathing.

*One-elephant, two-elephant, three-elephant, four-elephant. . .* I counted the seconds in my head, trying to figure out how long they were both unconsciously holding their breaths for.

I mean, I was pretty sure that you can get brain damage from lack of oxygen, but I didn't know how long it would take for that to happen. I thought about going over to ask the St John's Ambulance people, but by the time I got back the damage would be done and my two friends would be either dead or in a vegetative state. (At that moment, I was very glad I'd never been in love yet – it looked like it could seriously damage your health.)

I was just about to slap them on the back to shock them into taking a breath when a voice boomed from the stage.

"Welcome to this year's Rock The Park festival!" said some bloke in an old Rolling Stones T-shirt (the one with the tongue and lips on it). "Are you ready to do some dancing?"

A mixed roar of "Yes!!!"s and rude yells answered back.

"Come on, I want to see everyone on their feet for the first band of the day – give a big welcome to Scooter!!"

As one, the crowds shuffled up.

I heard Sylv and Becca both take deep breaths as they pushed themselves on their feet, so – phew – I could relax, they weren't about to die on me. Still, it didn't matter what the bloke doing the introductions said, I wouldn't be dancing. Not in public. My dancing was strictly done behind closed doors, with only the rescue toys as my audience.

"Hello!! How you all doing!" a different voice suddenly boomed from the stage.

"Is that that Ade guy?" Becca whispered, returning to normal now that my brother was out of sight, presumably in the wings of the big stage.

"Yep," I whispered back.

There Ade was, centre stage, looking floppier than ever, giving a wave to the crowd. The boy Sylv couldn't help loving, just the same as Becca couldn't help aching over Jo-Jo, the same as Dad couldn't help falling for

Nina, the same as I couldn't help missing my father so much it hurt.

I didn't know for sure, but I had a feeling Sylv was holding her breath again, in case Ade glanced at the sea of faces in front of him and spotted her among them. (Possibly not that hard, as she'd be the only one with white make-up, black lipstick and newly dyed streaks of scarlet in her hair.) She'd be holding her breath, waiting for the band to play "her" song, and hoping – I bet – that Ade might introduce it by saying something like, "I wrote this about very special girl, who I wish I hadn't let go. . .".

But that wasn't about to happen, not straightaway, at least.

"OK, we're called Scooter," Ade carried on booming, "and here we go!"

It only took about ten seconds for the crowd to get it, to fall for the thundering drums, the infectious bass, the rhythmic guitar and the fantastic, edge-of-croaky vocals.

"This is great!" Becca burbled in my ear, as we stood on our tiptoes to see above the bouncing, bobbing crowd of newly devoted fans during the first track, called something like, "The Future Is Now". I didn't know that one, or any of their songs apart from that snatch of chorus I'd heard on Jo-Jo's i-Pod the other day.

"He's good, isn't he?" Sylv said shyly, during the second track they played ("Mission To Matter"), as if she was a burstingly proud mum at her kid's school show.

"Definitely!" I had to admit, now that I was seeing a sparklier side to Floppy Ade I was sort of *starting* to appreciate why Sylv might have fallen for him in the first place.

And then it all went – how can I put it? – *wrong*.

"Cheers!" said Ade, as the roars and clapping rang out at the end of that second track. "Now we're gonna do a song called 'So Sorry, Sylvia' –"

Me, Sylv and Becca: the three of us gasped as one.

"– it's about this nutty goth girl I used to go out with. I know – a goth! Don't hold it against me!"

Gulp.

I somehow didn't think it was *quite* what Sylv had been hoping to hear. And I didn't think she needed or deserved to have a few faces turn round in her direction and snigger.

"They don't know it's about *you*!" I tried to say supportively.

"Yeah," Becca chipped in. "They're only looking at you because Ade's slagging off goths in general!"

Eek – an epic clunker from my best friend there.

Sylv, meanwhile, looked like all the blood had drained from her body, and it wasn't just the white make-up that was doing it. She knew what the words were about – she'd heard them close up and personal before. Only maybe not preceded by quite such a horrible, callous, unfeeling introduction.

*"'You're into stuff I can't get my head around,*
*The way you like to look I just don't get,*
*You're into me much more than I'm into you,*
*I think it would be better if we'd never met.*
*So, sorry, Sylvia, but me and you are through.*
*So, sorry, Sylvia, it's not me, it's you. . .'"*

As the band brashly started thundering out their song, I realized that Sylv was in desperate need of a) escape, b) somewhere to sit before her legs gave way.

"Right – we're going," I muttered, putting an arm around Sylv's waist and steering her through a crush of bodies towards the nearby park gate, and the nearby café I'd gone to with Dad

Becca followed right behind, saying her polite little "excuse me"s as we struggled our way out.

When we finally pushed through the throng, I took a peek at Sylv and gasped. It looked like her face had *melted*. Smoky black eyeshadow was streaking into white face paint, and patches of proper pink skin were showing where the tears of a goth had washed the make-up away to reveal Sylv's true colours.

Speaking of true colours, I think Ade had just shown his. But at least him being completely and totally awful about her did Sylv a favour, in a way. He'd more or less switched off her Loving Him Button for *good*. There'd be no more stalking and hoping. She could just be free of him, and the other useless blokes in her life (her faraway-in-Spain dad, her mum's dangerous-dog-loving boyfriend) and start her shiny new life with her stint at Camp America, and then off to uni in Southampton

"*You* take Sylv to the loo and sort her out," I said to Becca, as we stood by the park gate and waited for a gap in the traffic, so we could cross to the café. "*I'll* get us some coffees."

Three seconds and a lot more make-up damage later, I pushed the café door open and pointed the girls in the direction of the toilets. Then I turned around, to see which of the heather-decorated tables I could claim as ours. Mum had given me quite a lot of money today – I was meant to pick up several cartons of orange juice for the sangria Krystyna was making for the party on the way home – but I could blow some of it now on great slabs of comforting chocolate cake. I was sure even the St John's Ambulance team would say that was medicinal, in the circumstan—

"Heather!"

Freeze-frame the moment, in vivid detail:

Dad.

Dad sitting at the same window seat *we* had.

[*He must be living round here, if this was his local café.*]

Dad facing me. Nina spinning her long, red hair around to see me.

[*Close up, she was prettier than when I last saw her, barfing on Dad's shoes.*]

What was I going to do, what was I going to do, what was I going to do? I panicked.

[*I wasn't exactly ready to act all friendly and cosy with them yet, not by about a million miles.*]

And then I saw something.

[*A something that wouldn't normally have registered on my radar. No way.*]

It was a magazine on the table between them. A magazine called *Pregnancy & Birth*.

[*The other week, something more important than me had made Dad cut short our "reunion". What had he said on his mobile again? Something about, "Are you sure?", before his face paled, then reddened, like he'd had some kind of shock. Maybe someone telling him they thought they were pregnant?*]

"It's more complicated than you think," he'd written in one of his emails. And then there was the barfing. Morning sickness, it was called, though Mum once said it didn't just happen in the morning.]

"Heather. . .?"

The look in his eyes, the tone of his voice, the way he leaped up and over to me. He knew I knew.

"Heather, it's all happened really suddenly for us. We didn't plan it. And Nina never thought she'd be able to have kids, so we couldn't tell anyone till the doctors let us know if everything was all right. Heather? *Heather!!!*"

Before he could hurt me any more, I bolted, leaving a hole where my heart should be and a goth in the toilet . . .

From: **wombat**

Subject: **Bye**

Date: **Saturday 28 May**

To: **rsmith@smiledentalgroup**


Dad –

Stuff you need to know:

Jo-Jo's not going to be a dentist – he's going to be a band manager.

Tallie might seem slightly kooky but I'm pretty sure she's having a lot more fun since you've been gone.

I can see Mum downstairs in the party in the garden now, and she's doing a very sexy dance with a very handsome man.

And as for me, I don't think there's any point in keeping in touch any more, do you?

Have a nice life.

Heather

## 100% random imperfectness

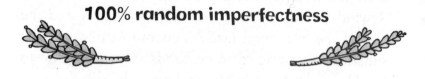

The noseless tiger perched on the top of my computer stared at me sympathetically, like it understood my dilemma.

Well, it *had* been listening to me having the same, two-word argument with myself for the last ten minutes.

*Saturday 18.05*

The time on my computer screen. Time for the party in the garden to gear up. Time to zap the angry email to Dad.

"Send," I muttered to myself, or more precisely, the finger that was hovering over the paper-plane icon.

"Or delete. . .?" I mumbled, my finger edging over to the red no-go circle.

The icon I *really* wished was on my menu bar was an icon to rewind; maybe some tiny, golden arrow that would magic away the last four hours. I'd happily press that. I'd like it to be 14.07, when Scooter were about halfway through their second song. Then I could fake a fainting fit and have my friends help me to the safety of the first aid tent. I'd let the St John's Ambulance people fan me and give me cold water or whatever, and then stage a miraculous recovery *just* as Scooter were finishing their set.

Shazam! Sylv wouldn't have heard how Ade had introduced *that* song, and be hurt and humiliated by it.

And in this wonderfully rewound world, there'd be no cafés, no unexpected, depressing surprises. Nope, in Rewind World, me, Sylv and Becca would spend the rest of the afternoon lazily mooching around in the sunshine, listening to more bands till it was time to head home and join in Mum's dippy salsa party.

I could be happily flitting around in the garden right now, helping set out the pitchers of sangria and bowls of olives, instead of sitting here in my room, weighed down by Dad's bump of a secret, stressing out about how the rest of my family would take the news. . .

"Should I tell them? When will I tell them?" I asked the noseless tiger, who didn't know where its own nose was, let alone the answer to my question.

"Maybe you should talk to Jo-Jo first?" Becca had suggested earlier, as we huddled in my room with Sylv and moped, in quiet whispers, so the secret would stay with me and not leak out to Mum and Tallie, happily preparing for the party. Becca and Sylv: they'd been great; I'd phoned them in the loo of the café, and they'd come running after me down the street, as soon as Sylv had washed enough of the ruined make-up off her face so she didn't frighten any small children. Becca said Dad had vanished by the time they'd come out into the main space of the café; him and Nina had gone back to their nearby love nest to choose cute borders for the nursery, probably. . .

"Jo-Jo will figure something out," Becca had added assuredly.

Ha.

The idea of telling Jo-Jo the news made my head melt.

He was already so angry with Dad that I thought this could tip him over the edge. I half-imagined him storming down to the surgery and whumping his disused squash racquet over Dad's head. Either that, or he'd get Ade to write a song called "Dad, I Hate You", and make sure it got to Number One in the charts, just to spite him.

"No, you should tell your mum, definitely," Sylv had said, her make-up re-plastered and immaculate again. She was so sweet; she'd put her own problems aside to make room for mine.

"Maybe," I'd murmured. "But not today. . . I'll let Mum have fun at her party first."

The party. Exactly what I *wasn't* in the mood for.

I rose slightly and peered down into the garden that was filling up steadily with dance-class friends of Mum's. Speaking of Mum, I could see Sylv helping her hang up a set of fairy lights across the trellis – the chilli peppers from the hall – all ready to switch on and glow brightly when dusk eased along later.

Becca was probably still in the kitchen, where she'd been helping Krystyna sort out nachos and guacamole.

"Are you OK?" Becca had asked, spotting me heading for the stairs not so long ago.

"I'm fine – I'm just nipping up to the loo," I'd lied, watching Krystyna watching me, narrow-eyed. Immediately, I'd slapped a beaming, fake smile on my face – the last thing I wanted was for her to go spoiling Mum's party by telling her something was wrong with me.

Send.

Delete.

Send.

Delete.

As I dithered some more, I twirled the ring on the red ribbon that was dangling from the desk lamp. Spin, spin, twirled the pearl ring, glinting in the light.

Words, words, I suddenly noticed, pulling the ring close to read the tiny inscription I'd just spotted inside. . .

*"Will ye go, lassie go?"*

Was it a line of poetry or something? It seemed kind of familiar. No – it wasn't from a poem, it was from a song . . . the song the old ladies in the charity shop had warbled when they'd heard my name.

*Click!*

With one flick of my finger, I closed up the email, and went straight on to i-Tunes, searching around for the track Jeannie and what's-her-name had said was called "Wild Mountain Thyme". As the computer did its search thing, I reached for the *British Book of Hit Singles and Albums* and flicked to "W" like a girl possessed.

And I *was* possessed, suddenly flooded with the romantic notion of some Scotsman who loved his dancing Pearl, but who knew that she was too scared to take the leap and travel the world with him. And so he'd had that snatch of lyric delicately etched into the ring he'd given her, hoping they'd be magic words; that they'd make Pearl brave enough to come with him to far-flung where-evers. . .

But there's no such thing as magic. And no such thing as an entry for "Wild Mountain Thyme" in my book, so no one had ever had a big hit with this old-time folk song.

I smiled to myself, thinking of how Pearl had got inside my head. "You can love different people in different ways"; that's what she'd said, when she was talking about her beloved husband and the fiancé she never saw again. Now I was going to have to get used to loving different people in different ways too. . . .

"What're you doing?" asked Tallie, shuffling across the room towards me in a pair of Mum's high heels held in place with red elastic bands discarded by our postman.

"Trying to figure out which finger to wear this on," I told her, as I untied the red ribbon and began testing out each finger for the best fit.

"What're you listening to?" she asked, leaning an elbow on the desk and tilting her head towards the tiny desk speakers that Dad had bought me last Christmas. I noticed she'd drawn a daisy chain around her wrist in red pen. She had a matching daisy doodled on her cheek.

"Just some song," I said with a shrug, as the sentimental drift of "Wild Mountain Thyme" played softly in the background.

"Are you coming down?" said my sister, already bored of my reply to her question. Tiago was suddenly at her feet, trying to lick her and trip her up with affection at the same time.

"In a little while."

"You have to come now, Heather."

"Why?"

"Because Mum and Krystyna are wondering where you are, and they can't do the surprise till you get downstairs, and I need some cake."

"What are you on about, Tallie? What surprise?" I asked.

"It's your birthday!"

"It's not, Tallie! Mine is on the. . ." I couldn't bring myself to mention the real date of my dumb birthday. "My birthday was ages ago!"

"Yeah, but Mum forgot. So she decided today that she wanted this party to sort of be your birthday party too. Like a *token* birthday, she said, same as you did for Tiago!"

Squidge.

The sound of my whole being turning to mush.

I stood up again and peered down into the garden, where I could see a newly arrived Jo-Jo, laughing and dancing with a girl on each arm; one a dramatic goth and the other a pink-cheeked, love-struck Becca. Sylv glanced up and waved at me. She looked . . . all right. Maybe the stuff with Ade was for the best, in a weird way. Maybe it had broken the spell she was under. She might need to get herself a new hobby now – hopefully, one that didn't involve stalking.

And there was Krystyna, clearing a space (for a birthday cake?) on the garden table. She took a handful of what looked like tiny candles out of her pocket.

"Heather?"

It was Mum's voice, drifting up the stairs.

"Shh! Don't tell about the surprise!" Tallie suddenly urged me, getting everything back to front.

"Hi, honey!" said Mum, appearing at my bedroom door like a blast of summer warmth in her red top and the flower tucked behind her ear.

Tallie and Tiago wriggled by her, heading off down the stairs like a couple of pups.

"What made you vanish up here?" Mum asked.

"Um, I was just going to look up sites about Mexico, for our holiday," I said, trotting out the first lie that came to mind. I was about to follow it up with some truth, and show Mum the inscription inside Pearl's pearl, when she interrupted me.

"I see. I thought you might have come up here because you were feeling bad about what happened with your dad today."

Shock sucked the words right out of my head. How did she *know*?!

"Becca just told me."

Ah, Becca. My best friend had been blabbing again, only to *my* mother this time, instead of her own. She owed me one big, enormous, embarrassed sorry for that. . .

"She was worried about you. And then I just checked my mobile and realized your dad's left me a whole pile of messages. Guess he was worried about you being upset, too."

*Me* upset? What about *Mum*? I examined her face for signs of emotional damage; I couldn't bear for her to be hurt, or for the hibernation to start again.

But bizarrely, she looked . . . well, like Sylv. Not a *goth*, I mean. She looked all right, was what I am trying to say.

"It's fine, Heather," Mum said, putting her hand over mine. "I knew all about the baby already – your dad called me earlier in the week. He wanted everything out in the open."

"That must have been fun for you," I said, slipping into the comfort of black humour.

"I've had better phone calls," she said with a wry smile and a shrug. "We've spoken a few times since then, trying to decide on how and when to tell the three of you."

"And when *were* you going to tell us?" I quizzed her.

"We still hadn't quite worked that out yet," said Mum in a tone of voice that made me suspect the conversations my parents were having weren't exactly at the totally amicable stage yet.

Still, at least they were *talking*, and at least I didn't have the bump secret weighing me down any more (actually, I might have to give Becca a big hug for blurting later). Now it was Mum's secret too.

"But let's not spoil the party. We'll talk about – we'll *all* talk about – it later, yes?" said Mum, holding out a hand to me. "So come on downstairs and dance with me. . ."

I nearly reminded her that I didn't dance in public, but then I remembered that the dancing part was a ruse; she was still hiding the fact that I was about to have a surprise birthday sprung on me.

"I'll come in two minutes, I promise," I told her. "Let me log off here first."

Mum nodded and left me to it, probably hurtling downstairs to get the candles lit and everyone ready to sing.

Which left me with a moment to think, and an email to send.

The thinking part went like this. . .

For twelve years, I'd felt like the odd one out in my

small, neat, perfect family. But my family didn't remotely resemble the way it looked three short months ago. Back then, it was just Mum, Dad, son, daughter and wombat. And now? Now it seemed to consist of:

- A salsa-ing, thirty-seven-year-old teenager
- An eyeliner-wearing, rock 'n' roll rebel
- A beautiful gremlin child
- An exotically named dopey dog
- A goth who kept nail varnish in the fridge
- A strange but loyal Polish person
- A noseless tiger and his fifty-one furry friends
- A fascinating (if not very alive) great-gran, who I was suddenly very proud and excited to be named after
- Not to mention a future half-brother or sister (and Dad, and, er, Nina, I supposed)

Basically, my family was now a sprawling, rambling mess of 100% random imperfectness – and I belonged in it *perfectly*.

What an excellent present for my token thirteenth birthday. . .

And as for the email?

I moved the arrow to the right spot, and bang – *Delete*.

Before I went downstairs, all ready to be surprised, I wanted to bash out another email in its place.

And if I wrote it quickly enough, I might have time to borrow some pretty, purple nail varnish from the fridge and glam myself up for my big "surprise". . .

**From:** Pearlgirl

**Subject:** An Urgent Message of Wowness

**Date:** Saturday 28 May

**To:** rsmith@smiledentalgroup

Hi Dad

Hope you didn't get confused by my new email name.

Anyway, about today – I just wanted to say wow. Like, *wow*.

I think I'm going to be *very* excited and happy for you, but I'll have to take it slowly. Jo-Jo and Tallie will be the same, but it might take a bit longer with them. And, hey, there's no rush.

I have to go – Mum's made today my "token" birthday, since my old one is so rubbish.

Got to blow out a candle and make a wish (to see you soon, *properly*, maybe?).

Love

Heather x

PS I just looked in the *British Book of Hit Singles and Albums* to see what my new "token" birthday song is. It's "Come On You Reds" by Manchester United Football Club, which is *quite* a lot worse and even more dumb than "Doop" by Doop. Just my luck. . .